Books by

Historical Western Romance Series

MacLarens of Fire Mountain

Tougher than the Rest, Book One
Faster than the Rest, Book Two
Harder than the Rest, Book Three
Stronger than the Rest, Book Four
Deadlier than the Rest, Book Five
Wilder than the Rest, Book Six

Redemption Mountain

Redemption's Edge, Book One
Wildfire Creek, Book Two
Sunrise Ridge, Book Three
Dixie Moon, Book Four
Survivor Pass, Book Five
Promise Trail, Book Six
Deep River, Book Seven
Courage Canyon, Book Eight
Forsaken Falls, Book Nine
Solitude Gorge, Book Ten
Rogue Rapids, Book Eleven, Coming next in the series!

MacLarens of Boundary Mountain

Colin's Quest, Book One,
Brodie's Gamble, Book Two
Quinn's Honor, Book Three
Sam's Legacy, Book Four
Heather's Choice, Book Five
Nate's Destiny, Book Six
Blaine's Wager, Book Seven
Fletcher's Pride, Book Eight, Coming next in the series!

Contemporary Romance Series

MacLarens of Fire Mountain

Second Summer, Book One
Hard Landing, Book Two
One More Day, Book Three
All Your Nights, Book Four
Always Love You, Book Five
Hearts Don't Lie, Book Six
No Getting Over You, Book Seven
'Til the Sun Comes Up, Book Eight
Foolish Heart, Book Nine
Forever Love, Book Ten, Coming next in the series!

Peregrine Bay

Reclaiming Love, Book One, A Novella
Our Kind of Love, Book Two

Burnt River

Shane's Burden, Book One by Peggy Henderson
Thorn's Journey, Book Two by Shirleen Davies
Aqua's Achilles, Book Three by Kate Cambridge
Ashley's Hope, Book Four by Amelia Adams
Harpur's Secret, Book Five by Kay P. Dawson
Mason's Rescue, Book Six by Peggy L. Henderson
Del's Choice, Book Seven by Shirleen Davies
Ivy's Search, Book Eight by Kate Cambridge
Phoebe's Fate, Book Nine by Amelia Adams
Brody's Shelter, Book Ten by Kay P. Dawson
Boone's Surrender, Book Eleven by Shirleen Davies
Watch for more books in the series!

The best way to stay in touch is to subscribe to my newsletter. Go to www.shirleendavies.com and subscribe in the box at the top of the right column that asks for your email. You'll be notified of new books before they are released, have chances to win great prizes, and receive other subscriber-only specials.

Blaine's Wager

MacLarens of Boundary Mountain

Historical Western Romance Series

SHIRLEEN DAVIES

Book Seven in the MacLarens of Boundary Mountain Historical Western Romance Series

Avalanche Ranch Press, LLC
PO Box 12618
Prescott, AZ 86304

Blaine's Wager is a work of fiction. Names, characters, places, and incidents are either products of the author's imagination or used fictitiously. Any resemblance to actual events, locales, or persons, living or dead, is wholly coincidental.

Book design and conversions by Joseph Murray at 3rdplanetpublishing.com

Cover design by Kim Killion, The Killion Group

ISBN: 978-1-941786-77-2

I care about quality, so if you find something in error, please contact me via email at shirleen@shirleendavies.com

Description

Blaine's Wager, Book Seven, MacLarens of Boundary Mountain Historical Western Romance Series

Blaine MacLaren yearns to be a man his family considers a strong leader. After a lifetime living in his older brother's shadow, his uncles finally give him the chance he craves—running their new properties near Settlers Valley. Embracing the challenge, he rides away from Circle M with only one regret—leaving the woman he desires more than he cares to admit.

Lia Jacobs has been running for four years, staying a few towns ahead of the family who plans to drag her home. Landing in Conviction, she believes herself safe, until a wildly handsome man turns her dreams upside down.

Beginning to trust him and forging a friendship, she starts to think a future, maybe even love, is possible. Then he rides away, leaving her alone with shattered dreams and a bruised heart.

The days are long, the nights longer as Blaine works to keep the woman he'd left behind from his thoughts. Nothing helps, until a series of threatening events forces him to focus on the ranch and not the throbbing pain in his chest.

Lia buries herself in her work, forgetting the danger of staying in one place too long. The arrival of those who search for her forces Lia to make a tough decision—one taking her away from a known danger and into the path of another.

She may have outsmarted those who chase her. But is exchanging one type of threat for another, one endangering her heart, any better?

Blaine's Wager, book seven in the MacLarens of Boundary Mountain Historical Western Romance Series, is a stand-alone, full-length novel with an HEA and no cliffhanger.

Book 1: Colin's Quest
Book 2: Brodie's Gamble
Book 3: Quinn's Honor
Book 4: Sam's Legacy
Book 5: Heather's Choice
Book 6: Nate's Destiny
Book 7: Blaine's Wager

Visit my website for a list of characters for each series.
http://www.shirleendavies.com/character-list.html

Acknowledgements

Many thanks to the wonderful members of my Reader Groups. Your support, insights, and suggestions are greatly appreciated. And as always, a huge thank you to my husband who is my greatest fan.

As always, many thanks to my editor, Kim Young, proofreader, Alicia Carmical, Joseph Murray, who is superb at formatting my books for print and electronic versions, and my cover designer, Kim Killion.

Blaine's Wager

Chapter One

Blaine knew it was a bad idea from the beginning.

Lying flat on his back, he stared up at the hole in the floor of the barn's loft. Warning bells had sounded in his head the instant he'd put his boot on the sagging planks. He should've stepped back, tested the floor by setting one of the bales onto the weakened section.

Now his head throbbed and back ached to the point he didn't want to sit up. He could almost picture his cousin, Heather, staring down, calling him an eejit before reaching out a hand to help him up.

The last had Blaine forcing himself into a seated position, knees drawn up, arms resting over them. Heather and her husband, Caleb, would be arriving any moment to help clean out and repair the barn. Under no circumstances could he let them see him on the ground, covered in a disgusting mixture of manure, hay, and dirt.

Hearing the sound of approaching horses, Blaine hastened to stand, groaning at the slice of pain in the back of his head. Cursing himself as a fool, he brushed off what he could, spotting his hat several feet away. Grabbing it, he settled it on his head seconds before Caleb and Heather reined up outside the barn doors.

Heather stared at him a moment, glancing up to see the hole in the loft floor. Shaking her head, she slid to the ground. "Eejit. You couldn't wait a wee bit for us to get here and help you." She looked at Caleb. "I told you the lad would do something foolish if we didn't get here soon."

Masking a grin, Caleb dismounted, studying the broken planks. Walking directly under the gaping hole, he shrugged. "Seems we'll need to replace the entire floor before doing anything else. Do you have the boards?"

Blaine thought of the stack of old lumber out back. "Not enough. I'll be needing to make a trip to town once we've a list of supplies. Nails, hammer, shovel, broad axe..." His voice faded when he placed fisted hands on his waist and stared up at the splintered planks. "I'd best be getting a wagonload of wood. I'll need to borrow your wagon, Caleb."

"I plan to go to town with you. We'll stop at our ranch and get it."

Heather walked around the barn for the first time since the MacLarens completed the purchase of this ranch, as well as a few other properties not far from Settlers Valley. A few hours' ride from Conviction, Blaine had been selected as the foreman of the expanded ranch.

"It's not a bonny sight."

Blaine brushed hay from his shirt, his gaze narrowing as he looked around. "Nae, it isn't."

She rested a hand on her protruding stomach, a grin curving the corners of her mouth. "We'll have it cleaned up and looking grand in no time."

Blaine picked up a broken shovel, tossing it atop the pile of trash in a corner. "Just don't be working too hard, Heather. You've a wee bairn to think about."

"Ach. The bairn won't be coming for months."

Caleb dragged a splintered sawhorse across the ground, dropping it in front of Blaine. "I can fix this for you. Maybe some of the tools, as well." He looked at Heather. "As long as you promise not to overdue yourself. It's going to take us most of the day to get to town and back." Walking to her, he placed his hands on her shoulders. "It would be better for you to ride with us as far as our ranch and stay there today. If Blaine agrees, we'll get supplies and return there for the night. We'll return early tomorrow morning with everything we need."

She looked at her cousin. "We'd be leaving the ranch without anyone here, Blaine."

He threw his head back, laughing. "Ah, lass. There's nothing to take. The house, barn, and bunkhouse are almost falling down. We've moved the cattle and horses to your ranch until the ranch hands from Circle M arrive." Blaine gestured around the open space. "Would you be seeing anything of value?"

Leaning against Caleb's shoulder, she shook her head, a wry grin spreading across her face. "Nae. Even the pitchfork is broken. Is the house as bad?"

Blaine grimaced. "Almost. They took all the furniture, food, and supplies. I've been sleeping on my bedroll. The ranch hands are bringing furniture."

Walking to the door of the barn, she looked at the other buildings. "Will they be needing to build their own cots for the bunkhouse?"

Blaine joined her, recalling what he'd seen. "Nae. The bunks are fine. The benches and table are damaged. There'll be plenty of work for them when they arrive."

Caleb moved next to them. "When do you expect them?"

"This week." Blaine quirked a brow. "Which isn't soon enough."

Highlander Ranch
Caleb's Ranch near Settlers Valley

"Keeping the boys in jail overnight inconvenienced me more than them." Nate stabbed another piece of beef, putting it into his mouth.

Blaine looked between him and his new bride, Geneen, who was as close to him as a sister. "Meaning you weren't able to ride back to the ranch and your wife."

Nate swallowed, his lips twisting in disgust. "I didn't sleep at all. The boys couldn't keep their mouths shut, and the cot in the last jail cell is horrible. Something else to replace."

"Why?" Caleb asked. "They're mostly used for prisoners, right?"

"True, but there'll be times when either George or I will have to stay overnight."

Caleb cocked his head to the side. "George? Do you mean the young man who helped Colt guard the gold wagon?"

"The same. He didn't want to work for Leland Nettles at the Acorn Mine anymore, and I needed a deputy. He started this morning."

Geneen shot a pleased look at Heather. "Nate gave him the use of his room at Mrs. Keach's boardinghouse. There shouldn't be many nights when Nate will have to stay in town."

Caleb pushed his empty plate away. "With the previous sheriff gone, most of the crime seems to have disappeared."

Nate nodded. "No one knew the full extent of his crimes until the man's death."

A wicked gleam appeared in Heather's eyes. "Mrs. Keach told me it should've come a long time ago. She wishes she'd been the one to do it."

Geneen bit her lower lip to hide her amusement, glancing at Nate.

"Mrs. Keach has an opinion on everything, Heather." Crossing his arms, Nate leaned back in his chair. "She's got a heart of gold, but I wouldn't want to cross her."

Nate had gotten to know the older widow who owned the boardinghouse while he lived in town and worked for Marcus Kamm, the blacksmith. Ignoring the fact the woman created as much gossip as she passed along, Nate found her to be loyal, honorable, and one of the best cooks around.

"The last time I was in town, she was in the general store, telling Mr. Beall how she shot a man for trying to slip out without paying for room and board. Got him right in the, well...in his buttocks." Geneen put a hand over her mouth to stifle the giggles.

Heather didn't bother to hide her delight, bursting into laughter. "She is a bonny woman."

Watching the joy on the women's faces, the corners of Nate's eyes crinkled. Shifting, he looked at Blaine, noticing the distant expression on his face, realizing how quiet his friend had been. Lowering his voice, he leaned toward him.

"Are you thinking of the young lady in Conviction?"

Blaine jerked to attention. "What do you mean?"

Nate shrugged. "Brodie sent me a telegram about a group of rustlers who might be headed this way. He also said a lady named Lia asked about you."

Staring at his empty plate, Blaine shifted in his seat, feeling a strong urge to get up and leave. "She's a lass I met before moving up here. Sweet and..." A hint of a smile curved his lips as an image of Permilia Jacobs entered his mind.

"Bonny?" Nate prodded.

His features softened. "Aye. Quite bonny." Pushing his chair away from the table, Blaine stood. "You lasses have done enough for one day. I'll help with the dishes tonight."

Heather shook her head. "Nae, Blaine. You've a long day ahead of you tomorrow and I've a long way to go before I'm too big to help in the kitchen." She glanced at Caleb. "I'll bring coffee to you in the study."

"Blaine's right. You've done enough." Caleb stood, putting an arm around her waist. "I can see you're tired. The boys and I will clean up tonight. You and Geneen head upstairs. We won't be down here long." Kissing her forehead, he spun her toward the stairs. "Just stay awake until I get up there."

Looking over her shoulder, Heather shot him a wicked smile. "Ah, lad, you know I'll wait for you."

Blaine listened to their banter, so much like his older brother, Colin, and his wife, Sarah. It was the way of the MacLaren family. Their homes had always been full of love and mischief, loyalty and laughter. Hearing their teasing never bothered him before. Tonight, he felt a stab of melancholy, which troubled him more than a little bit.

"Goodnight to you, Heather."

She stopped next to Geneen, who'd just hugged Nate. "Goodnight to you, too, Blaine. I'll be seeing you in the morning. Oh, and thank you for cleaning the kitchen."

Chuckling, he shook his head. "Don't be getting used to it, lass. And don't be running back downstairs if you hear anything break."

Crossing her arms, she glared at him in mock anger. "Don't you be making me mad, Blaine. Even in my condition, I'd still take you."

A wide grin slashed across his face, his hands raising in defense. "And I've no doubt you'd whip me good."

Caleb clasped him on the shoulder. "Enough, you two." Turning him around, he shoved Blaine toward the kitchen, winking at Heather.

Nate watched the women walk up the stairs, heads together, whispering in the way he'd become accustomed to seeing. Stacking the dirty dishes, he drew in a deep breath, looking into the open kitchen door.

He'd never seen Blaine show any emotion about a woman outside the family. Never heard of him holding an interest in any female. Colin had once said ranching was his brother's only love. Everyone had said the same about Quinn, until Emma changed his mind.

Nate thought of the woman in Brodie's message, wondering if there was more to it than Blaine wanted to admit. If so, he felt a stab of discomfort for his friend. Nate knew what it was like to be separated from the woman you cared about, believing no way existed for you to ever come together.

Watching through the open doorway as Caleb and Blaine tossed water at each other, Nate shoved thoughts of the mystery woman aside. Whatever was going on in his friend's life, it was none of his business. For that, he was thankful.

Conviction

"Lia, your order for Brodie's table is ready."

Permilia Jacobs blew an errant strand of hair from in front of her eyes, picking up three plates filled with potatoes, roast, and carrots. She knew Brodie MacLaren and the two deputies with him liked their meals hot. She didn't plan to disappoint them.

"Here you are, gentlemen." Setting the plates down, she took a careful look at Brodie's face, a pasty mixture of white and green. "Are you all right, Sheriff?"

Sam Covington, Brodie's brother-in-law and fellow lawman, barked out a laugh. "We just took Maggie to Doc Vickery."

"He threw me out." Brodie's broken expression made Lia want to wrap her arms around the stoic lawman.

"Doc didn't actually toss you out. He strongly suggested we take you for a drink or food." Seth Montero raised a brow, glancing at Lia. "I voted for drinks, but these two thought food would be best."

Lia grinned. "And they're right. The sheriff will need all the strength he can get once the baby comes."

She watched Brodie's throat work, a grimace on his face as he stared down at the food. "Would you like something else to eat, Sheriff? We have chicken soup, or the cook could make you some gruel."

Seth's brows furrowed. "Gruel?"

Holding up a hand, Brodie shook his head. "Nae. No soup or gruel for me, lass. If I can't be swallowing meat, I'll not be eating."

Seth looked up at Lia. "Gruel?"

"A thin porridge." When his expression didn't change, Lia pursed her lips. "You boil water or milk and add oats or wheat."

His eyes widened. "For feeding babies and old folks, right?"

Brodie glared at him, spearing a piece of roast and sticking it into his mouth. Chewing still came hard, though. The last image he had was of Maggie, her face red, forehead beaded with sweat, hands clutching her stomach. Pushing his plate away, he shoved back his chair.

"Oh no, you don't." Sam grabbed his arm. "Doc Vickery said he'd send word as soon as the baby comes. And Jinny is there with Maggie." Mentioning Brodie's sister calmed him a bit.

Seth snickered. "Don't make us lock you in the jail, Sheriff."

"This is not anything like when Colin and Sarah had Grant," Brodie grumbled, settling down in the chair.

"Grant was born at home, with all the women around to help. As I recall, Colin was with the men downstairs." Sam picked up his coffee, blowing across the top before taking a sip.

"They let him upstairs just before Grant was born." Brodie scrubbed a shaky hand down his face. Gripping the arms of the chair, he willed himself to take deep breaths. "Sam, you have a son. How long will this take?"

The amusement on Sam's face faded at the thought of how Robbie came into the world. "If you remember, I wasn't there."

Closing his eyes, Brodie nodded. "Aye. Sorry, lad."

The gloomy expression left Sam's gaze, replaced with understanding. "It will take as long as it takes. Jinny is there. You know she'll come get you as soon as the baby arrives."

"Some babies take an hour or two, others five times that long. I've seen some cause misery for two days before deciding to join the world."

Three pairs of eyes locked on Lia.

"You've helped with births?" Brodie asked.

Not realizing what she'd revealed until he called her on it, she nodded. "I have. Where I lived before there were many births...and deaths."

"You were a midwife?"

Licking her lips, she nodded at Brodie.

"And where was that, lass?"

Lia's heart stilled. She couldn't reveal more about her past, especially to a lawman. Swallowing, she cleared her throat, desperate to think of a way out of telling the truth.

Jinny came rushing through the door of the restaurant. "Brodie!" She dashed to their table. "You must come now."

Standing, his expression tight, he pushed the chair back so hard it tipped over. "Is Maggie all right?"

Gulping, Jinny's frightened gaze met her brother's. "The lass is bleeding. Both Doc Vickery and Doc Tilden are with her."

Brodie clutched her arm. "The bairn?"

"The laddie is fine. Gwen is with him."

Gwen Acheson worked at Buckie's Castle, a saloon in Conviction known for offering full drinks and beautiful women. Before being accepted to work as Doc Vickery's nurse, she'd initiated many young men on how to pleasure a woman—Colin, Quinn, Brodie, and Blaine being a few of them. The irony wasn't lost on Brodie.

"I've got to get to her." He grabbed his hat and sprinted out the door, Jinny a few paces behind.

Seth watched them go before looking at Sam. "I'll wait back at the jail."

Nodding, Sam reached into his pocket, pulling out enough money to cover all their meals. "This should take care of it."

Taking the money, Lia touched his arm. "Will you let me know what happens with Maggie?"

He glanced around the restaurant, seeing it almost empty. "Joe might let you come to the clinic. The docs might appreciate you being there."

Shaking her head, Lia backed away. "Oh, no. They wouldn't need help from me."

Spotting Joe across the room, Sam walked around Lia and right up to him. "Doc Vickery needs Lia's help at the clinic. Can you spare her for bit?" He winced at stretching the truth, telling himself it was for a good reason.

Joe's brows shot up, then lowered, noticing the number of empty tables. "Sure, Sam. It's not too busy tonight."

Shaking his hand, Sam returned to Lia. "Come on. Joe's fine with you being gone for a while."

"But—"

"Please, Lia. Vickery and Tilden are exceptional doctors. The fact you know Maggie and have had some good experience isn't going to hurt."

Letting out a shaky breath, she nodded. "If you think it might help her."

"We won't know until you get there, will we?"

Chapter Two

Brodie paced the length of the small waiting room, his gaze darting between the closed door, where Maggie hovered between life and death, and Gwen, who sat in a chair, rocking his baby boy. Twice, he'd tried to enter the room to be with his wife. Each time, Hugh Tilden took him by the arm, leading him back to the front area. The sight of Maggie's pale face and dull eyes stabbed through him, a memory he'd never be able to remove.

"How is she?" Sam stepped next to Brodie while Lia stood at the open door to the clinic, her gaze fixed on the baby in Gwen's arms.

Threading a hand through his hair, his features creased with worry, eyes stormy. "Ach. They won't let me see her." He whirled toward the door of the examination room. "Maggie's in there and I've no idea if she'll live or die."

Sam placed a hand on his shoulder. "They're doing all they can, Brodie."

"What if it's not enough?" His eyes filled with pain, voice breaking. "What if I lose the lass?"

Turning toward Lia, Sam nodded at the closed door. "Maybe they'll let Lia help. She's had some experience and knows Maggie."

Brodie's gaze shot to hers. "Would you give it a try, lass?"

Lia didn't feel worthy, yet couldn't ignore the pleading look in his eyes. "I'm not sure what I can do that the doctors can't."

Walking to her, Brodie took her hand. "They won't let me in there. You can be with her, hold her hand...talk to her." He glanced at the closed door, then back at Lia. "I'd be grateful, lass."

She didn't have it in her to refuse. "All right." Lia moved next to Gwen. "Do you think they'll let me in?"

Holding the baby close to her chest, Gwen met her gaze. "If you've had some experience, they might welcome another woman in there. This is the first time I've helped with a birth, so I have little to offer."

Biting her lip, Lia sent an anxious look at Brodie. "It would only be to comfort Maggie."

Gwen gave her a grim smile. "All you can do is try, Lia."

Sucking in a breath, she nodded, then stepped to the door and knocked.

When the door opened, she looked past Doc Tilden to see Maggie's pasty features. "Is there something you want, Miss Jacobs?"

Swallowing, she nodded. "I've had some experience as a midwife. Perhaps I could stay with Maggie."

He stepped aside. "Come in." Hugh Tilden spared a glance at Brodie before closing the door. "We've slowed the bleeding, but it hasn't stopped. I'd appreciate it if you'd talk to her. Maybe she'll respond to you."

"I'll do what I can." Moving to the edge of the bed, she noted the ashen look on Maggie's face, the dark red hair matted beneath her head, and her shallow breathing. Taking a hand in hers, she leaned down, her voice a mere whisper. "Maggie, it's Lia. Can you hear me?" When she didn't respond, Lia continued. "You've a beautiful baby boy. He has your fair complexion and Brodie's dark hair. Gwen is with him."

"Brodie..."

If Lia hadn't been a few inches from Maggie's face, she wouldn't have heard the soft comment.

"He's with your baby, Maggie. He wants to be in here with you, but the doctors thought it better for him to stay with the baby for now." She squeezed Maggie's hand. "The doctors need you to tell them if you're in pain." Lia glanced at them, then back at Maggie. "Are you in any pain?"

"Bro...die..."

The one broken word pierced Lia's chest, making her throat constrict. Clearing it, she leaned closer. "He'll be here as soon as he can, Maggie, then you can see your baby boy. He's so beautiful. Have you decided on a name?"

A few moments passed before her lips moved. "Name..."

"That's right. Do you know what you'll name your baby, Maggie?" Lia did her best to recall the lessons other midwives had taught her about women after childbirth. Using their name helped keep them with you and not drift off.

"Shaun..."

Lia's mouth curved into a smile as she squeezed her hand again. "Shaun is a perfect name." She looked at Hugh Tilden, a brow arching.

"I think we have the bleeding stopped. Keep talking to her while Doctor Vickery and I clean up, then you can get Brodie and the baby."

Lia continued to hold Maggie's hand as she spoke about working at the Gold Dust, the interesting people she'd met, and her desire to learn more about nursing. At this, she noticed Hugh turn toward her.

"Are you interested in being a nurse, Lia?"

She felt her face flush at the question. Lia hadn't spoken of her dream to anyone. "I know it's a foolish thought, Doctor Tilden."

"But it's what you want, isn't it?"

Letting out a shaky breath, she shrugged. "Since I was a young girl."

He offered her an encouraging smile. "When you have time, we'll have coffee at the Gold Dust and discuss that dream of yours."

A ball of yearning constricted her throat. All Lia could do was nod, turning away so he wouldn't see the moisture building in her eyes. "I'd like that, Doctor."

"I believe we're ready for Brodie and the baby. Would you mind getting them, Lia?"

"Not at all." Squeezing Maggie's hand once more, she straightened, a smile of hope and gratitude brightening her face. Stepping into the front, she walked up to Brodie. His gaze latched onto hers, fear still evident in his features.

"Is Maggie...is the lass...all right?" His voice broke on the last.

"She's awake and asking for you, Sheriff. And you can take Shaun in with you."

Confusion washed across his face before a relieved smile curved his lips. "Aye. I'll be taking the wee bairn in with me." Stepping next to Gwen, he took his son from her arms, cradling the tiny child to his large frame. Looking up, he didn't bother hiding the sheen of tears in his eyes.

Waiting until he walked into the examination room and closed the door, Lia glanced between Sam and Gwen. "I believe Maggie's going to be all right."

Standing, Sam took a couple steps closer. "I never doubted you'd help get her through this, Lia. Why don't you sit down and rest before going back to the Gold Dust?"

Swiping damp hair from her forehead, she shook her head. "I'd better get back. Joe was generous in letting me come here at all."

Gwen pushed up from her seat, touching Lia's arm. "You let Joe know he did a good thing, letting you come. I couldn't watch the baby and help with Maggie at the same time." She glanced at the closed door. "Brodie saved all his worry for his wife. He's one of the most resilient men I've ever met, but when it comes to Maggie, well..." Gwen shook her head.

Sam's eyes lit up. "He's like most men when it comes to their wives."

Lia couldn't embrace the same thoughts. She'd never seen her father's face soften or show a trace of love when he looked at her mother. The same as so many other families where she grew up, their bond had been built on mutual respect and similar goals. Love never played a role in their relationship. At least not from what Lia had ever seen.

"Let the sheriff and Maggie know how happy I am for them." Without a backward glance, she stepped outside, walking up the boardwalk to the restaurant.

Lia slowed her pace, thinking of Blaine and allowing a brief wave of longing to wash over her. It always happened when she thought of him. The only man she'd ever permitted herself to feel a connection with, talk to without wondering about his motives. Something about him had broken down the barriers she'd built since leaving home at seventeen. The years on her own taught her men had a reason for everything they did. Few offered help without expecting something in return.

She'd never witnessed it in Blaine. Perhaps, if he'd come into her life sooner, maybe...

Lifting her chin, she pushed away the fantasy spinning inside her head each day since he'd left for Settlers Valley. If he ever visited Conviction, Lia hoped he'd think of her, maybe come into the Gold Dust for a meal. She filed the thought in a special corner of her mind, right next to her dream of someday becoming a nurse.

Highlander Ranch

Nate and Geneen rode next to each other as they approached the house, smiles on their faces. They'd ridden from Settlers Valley with news they couldn't wait to share with Caleb and Heather. Stopping outside the barn, both slid to the ground, Nate taking the reins of the horses.

"You go on inside and give Heather the letter. I'll take care of Nomad and Gypsy."

She didn't argue, dashing across the open space and up the steps to the porch. Opening the door, Geneen looked around.

"Heather!"

"I'm in the kitchen."

Clutching the letter in her hand, Geneen moved through the house, entering the kitchen as Heather stirred a pot on the stove.

"I have news from Brodie." She waved the letter in the air.

Glancing over her shoulder, Heather smiled. "What does the lad say?"

"Maggie had a baby boy!"

Dropping the spoon next to the stove, Heather squealed. "That's grand news. What's his name?" She moved next to Geneen.

"Shaun."

Grabbing the letter from Geneen's hand, she scanned it, her enthusiasm beginning to wane. "Maggie almost didn't make it." Heather looked at Geneen, concern combined with fear causing her voice to shake. "Brodie says the doctors had a hard time stopping the bleeding."

Touching her arm, Geneen took the letter from her hand. "It doesn't mean you'll go through the same, Heather. Every birth is different."

Reaching out, Heather steadied herself against the counter. "I know. It's just..."

Geneen shifted to face her. "The letter is a reason to celebrate, not worry about what may or may not happen."

Resting a hand on her protruding stomach, Heather nodded. "Ach. You're right. If I'd known of the news earlier, I'd have made something special for dessert."

"The baked apple pudding from last night will be fine." Washing her hands, Geneen dried them as she looked out the window. "Where's Caleb?"

"He's working at Blaine's with the men who arrived from Circle M. Caleb says the place is looking real good. This will probably be the last day he'll have time to help them."

"Smells good in here, ladies." Nate moved behind Heather, looking over her shoulder. "Venison stew?"

"It is."

Taking a fork off the counter, he moved it toward the pot. "Perhaps I should try some to make sure—"

Heather swatted his hand away. "You'll be doing no such thing."

Laughing, Nate stepped away. "Is Caleb still at Blaine's?"

"Aye. He should be back anytime now. I told him to bring Blaine with him."

Placing a kiss on Geneen's cheek, he leaned against the counter. "It's doubtful we'll see Blaine for a while. He's determined to work from sunup to sundown now that the men are here."

"The lad will be needing more than three men for a spread that size. I thought the uncles would've sent more, or even had Fletcher or Bram come over."

Nate pulled plates down from the cupboard, handing them to Geneen. "With Caleb and Blaine gone, I'm surprised they could spare even three, Heather. Blaine asked me to post notices in town for more help. He's looking for at least three more men. Anyone interested is supposed to talk to me. So far, no one's come by the jail. I even posted a notice at the docks in case anyone arriving by steamship is looking. Most of the men coming upriver head straight to the Acorn Gold Mine."

Geneen walked back in from the dining room, taking the utensils Nate held out to her. "How long has it been posted?"

"A few days is all."

"It takes time to get the word out, Nate. I'm guessing within a couple weeks, you'll be sending more men out to see Blaine than he'll need."

"Let's hope so, Geneen." The sound of the front door closing and men's voices had Nate walking out to the dining room before calling over his shoulder. "Geneen, you'll need to set another plate. Blaine decided to return with Caleb for a good meal."

Taking off his hat and gunbelt, Blaine set them on hooks, a slight grin spreading across his face. "I couldn't face one more night of beans and biscuits."

"You've come on a good night, lad." Heather walked up to him, holding out the letter.

He held it in his hand a moment, then looked up at his cousin. "Good news?"

She nodded. "Grand news."

Unfolding it, he read partway down the page. "Maggie had a wee laddie."

"They named him Shaun," Heather said, pointing at a spot on the page.

"Aye, I see that." Blaine continued reading, his breath catching as he got near the end. "Lia..." he breathed out.

Heather looked at him. "What's that, lad?"

Reading over the last words again, he folded the letter, handing it back to her. "Brodie said Maggie had a hard time. They brought someone from the Gold Dust to help."

Heather nodded. "Aye. Brodie said the lass had been a midwife before. She held Maggie's hand, talked to her until the doctors stopped the bleeding." As had become a habit, she settled a hand on her stomach. "She sounds like a fine lass."

His voice softened. "She is."

Eyes widening, his cousin cocked her head. "Do you know her?"

Blaine looked at Nate, then Caleb, seeing smirks on each face. "Aye. We've met. I'm glad the lass could help Maggie." Letting out a weary breath, he moved toward the kitchen, needing to get off the subject of the woman he left behind in Conviction. "I'm starving. When do we eat?"

Chapter Three

Conviction

"I heard about what happened with Maggie MacLaren, Lia. Sounds like you did real good." Joe dried a large pot, setting it on a rack by the kitchen door of the Gold Dust. Pouring another cup of coffee, he leaned against the counter, glad the morning breakfast was behind them.

Feeling the heat rise up her neck and onto her face, she shrugged. "I didn't do much, Joe. Held Maggie's hand and kept talking to her. Anyone could've done what I did."

"That's not what Brodie and Sam are telling people. They say Maggie might not have made it if you weren't with her."

Her face twisted into a frown. "That's just not so. What I should've been doing is holding the new baby so Gwen could've been in there with Maggie."

Joe waved a hand through the air. "Gwen's a good woman with a big heart, but she's no nurse. Before Doc Tilden arrived, Doc Vickery hired her after some explosions injured folks around town. No one else volunteered to help except Gwen and a couple other ladies from Buckie's Castle. She's calm and does what she's told, but no more than that. Doesn't have any real interest in anything other than bandaging wounds."

Shaking out the damp towel, he slid it onto the new swing-arm rack he'd ordered from San Francisco. "Maybe you should be asking the doctors to let you work for them."

Fearing what he hadn't said, she walked toward him. "Are you saying you don't need me here any longer?"

"Not at all, girl. I don't see why you can't work here and help at the clinic. I bet they'd pay you, too."

The idea took hold for an instant before Lia realized how ridiculous the notion sounded. Why would two experienced doctors need someone of her limited experience? "I've mainly bandaged wounds and helped with childbearing. A few times I had to help when a fever went through the family." She clamped her mouth shut, hoping Joe hadn't noticed her choice of words. A few seconds passed before he turned toward her.

"You still got family, Lia?"

Licking her lips, she looked away, then back at him. "A few, but they live a long way from here."

"Is that where you learned so much about helping people?"

Feeling her body beginning to tremble, the same as it always did when she thought of what she'd left behind, Lia nodded. "Guess so. Someone was always sick or having a baby. It's the way of it where I come from."

"You've been here a while now, but I don't think you've ever said where you're from."

"Didn't I tell you I came here from Sacramento?"

Joe studied her face, knowing it wasn't the entire truth, deciding he'd let it go for now. Lots of people moved to Conviction to get away from their pasts. In most cases, it wasn't his business.

"Maybe you did. How old were you when you started helping out with those feeling poorly?"

Shrugging, Lia bit her lower lip. "Ten, maybe nine."

"Must've been one helluva large family."

She knew he couldn't imagine just how large. Some days, she found herself thinking of her brothers and sisters, wondering how they were doing, if they were married and had children of their own. Wondering if her father had accomplished with her younger sisters what he'd failed to with her. Perhaps she should've stayed, done more to help her younger siblings.

"I was the oldest." A frown creased her brow. She didn't know why the comment slipped out and wished she could take it back.

"Yep. I know how that is. I'm the oldest of five, and the only boy." Joe pulled utensils from a drawer, lining them up on the big table in the restaurant kitchen. "Stayed until the youngest sister got married."

Pulling her thoughts away from her troubled past, Lia looked at him. "Were you ever married?"

A chuckle burst from his throat. "After almost raising four younger sisters?"

"I suppose that means you weren't."

"And that would be right, girl. I'm as free as they come and like it that way." Grabbing a cast iron skillet, he set it on the table, making a hasty decision. "Do you mind keeping watch on the restaurant for a few minutes? I've got an errand to run."

She looked out the door to the empty dining room. "Now would be a good time."

"I won't be gone long."

Amusement crossed her face as she watched him hasten his steps out the front door. For a big man, both in height and girth, Joe moved fast. She wondered what had him rushing out at a time when he'd normally be getting food ready for the noon meal.

Shrugging, she grabbed a damp cloth. By the time he returned, she'd have the last couple tables cleaned and ready for the next rush of people. This was one of her favorite times in the restaurant. The lull gave her time to think, enjoy the few dreams she still had.

Right now, her mind focused on the conversation about training with the doctors. Lia thought about how much nursing she'd done for her family and their neighbors. Some nights, she wouldn't lay down until after dawn, exhausted from helping with another birth or sitting up with a sick child.

Her father allowed her two hours, then he'd prod her out of bed to complete her chores. Those days, her younger sisters had already finished the milking, leaving Lia to do the laundry and help their mother with the cooking. It seemed there was never time to do anything other than work around their farm. By the time each child turned nine, they'd gotten all the schooling their mother could manage. Afterward, they were on their own if they had a desire to learn more than planting, harvesting, and raising and slaughtering animals.

Her mother had often said *it was our way.* Lia cringed at the reminder of her mother's often spoken words. She'd never been a lazy child, shirking her chores to play by the creek or run through the fields. Still, Lia always wondered if there was more to life than the little they saw from the confines of the family's farm. At seventeen, she'd decided to find out for herself.

"Lia? You feeling all right?"

She shook her head, glancing around. At some point, she'd taken a seat in the dining room, allowing her reminiscing to take over. Standing, she straightened her shoulders.

"Sorry, Joe. I don't know what came over me."

"As long as you're feeling good enough to help prepare for the noonday crowd."

Nodding, she looked outside, seeing the street full and boardwalk crowded with people. "I'm good."

He turned toward the kitchen. "Sometime before the day is out, you and me need to have another talk."

Her breath hitching, Lia followed him into the kitchen. "Can't we talk now?"

"Nope. Too much to do. You come in here, oh, about three o'clock. The place will be quiet again and we can talk."

Thinking the worst, all she could do was nod before pulling out a sack of potatoes and setting it on the table. "I'll fix these."

Glancing over his shoulder, Joe nodded, the hint of a smile tilting the corners of his mouth.

Staring at the dirty plates on the last table in the empty dining room, Lia stretched her back. It had been busier than normal. Besides the arrival of the stagecoach, a steamship docked just before noon, letting off over fifty passengers. Many found their way to the Gold Dust.

Lia touched the pocket in her skirt, her spirits lifting at what she felt. It was the steamship passengers, those of means wearing fashionable clothing, who sometimes left additional money on the table.

She still remembered the first time it happened. Not long after she started working for Joe, an older, elegant man from New York had left extra money. When she'd chased him outside, attempting to return the extra change, he'd held up his hand, refusing to take it back. The man explained the custom of tipping to her, a concept she'd never heard about, but now welcomed whenever it occurred.

Picking up the dishes, she returned to the kitchen, steeling herself for whatever Joe had to say. He'd been unusually quiet since coming back from his errand, only speaking when an order was ready. A talkative boss, Lia knew his silence couldn't be good.

Setting the plates by the sink, she touched her pocket once more. At least she now had a little money to help her out if Joe decided he no longer required her help. As the only server, the idea seemed absurd. Still...

"You ready for our talk?" Joe leaned a hip against the large wooden table in the center of the kitchen, crossing his arms.

Mimicking his stance, Lia crossed her arms, leaning against the counter. "Yes."

"You know my errand this morning?"

Her gaze narrowed. "Of course."

"Do you want to know where I went?"

Most days, Lia could take his drawn-out explanations. Today wasn't one of them. "It's none of my business, Joe."

His eyes flashed with amusement. "Today it is. I talked with Doc Vickery about taking you on. Sort of an apprentice position."

Chest tightening, her eyes widened. "Apprentice?" Lia whispered.

"A student."

Blowing out a breath, she nodded. "I understand what an apprentice is, Joe. What I don't understand is why Doc Vickery would make such an offer."

"I explained all you'd done for your family, how you helped with illness and childbirth, and your desire to be a nurse. Seems he'd already spoken to Doc Tilden about how you'd helped with Maggie. They can't offer you any pay right now, but they'd be willing to train you...if you still have an interest."

She felt her mouth open, but couldn't seem to get her voice to work. Her mind whirled from the announcement at the same time a ball of excitement built in her chest.

"Lia, are you all right? You look a little pale."

Dropping her hands to her sides, she took a step toward him. "Do I get to keep my job here?"

Joe's brows drew together. "Of course you do. How would I get anything done without you?"

She nodded, still not quite comprehending. "And I can still live in the back room?"

Joe's features softened. "Nothing else changes, Lia. You'll be working a couple hours at the clinic each day, serving meals here, and serving drinks at Buckie's, if you want to."

She shook her head, not quite meeting his gaze, her breath short and ragged. "Buckie's hasn't needed me for a while now. I think it would be best to work here and the clinic." Lia looked at him. "Don't you think?"

Shrugging, Joe grinned. "Whatever you want, girl."

"Two hours every day?"

"That's what the doctors agreed to. I was thinking either between breakfast and dinner or dinner and supper."

"Whatever is best for you, Joe."

"Then we'll take it a day at a time. Vickery said they're flexible. Of course, I may have to hire another person. Been meaning to do it for a while now. You've been working yourself to death with the increase in people coming to the Gold Dust. I might even expand on out back, enlarge the dining room and add more hotel space upstairs." Scratching his chin, he seemed to think about it a moment, then nodded. "Yep. I think I'd best start thinking real seriously about it."

Unable to control the excitement any longer, she dashed up to Joe and wrapped her arms around his neck. "Thank you so much. I would never have found the courage to ask them myself."

Patting her back, Joe disengaged himself, feeling a little embarrassed. Stepping back, he ignored the tears streaming down her face.

"Lia, you deserve this. It's your chance to make that dream of yours come true. Don't waste it." Clearing his throat, he looked away. "Guess we'd better get supper started."

Swiping the moisture from her face, Lia allowed herself a tentative smile. "Want me to peel more potatoes?"

"Don't need any more for supper." Joe opened a drawer and pulled out a yellowed piece of paper, handing it to her. "I haven't made this in a long time."

Taking it from his hand, she glanced at it. "Gingerbread cake. I haven't made this for years."

"Good. We'll need three for the restaurant and one for you and me to split when we're done." Bending down, he pulled out the equipment needed. "Here you are." He turned his back to Lia, hiding a grin.

Staring down at the recipe, Lia blinked a few times, trying to get her eyes to focus. She couldn't stop her thoughts from shifting to tomorrow and her first day at the clinic.

Lia lost one fantasy when Blaine left Conviction for Settlers Valley. Thanks to Joe, she still had one more dream, and she meant to never let anyone steal it from her.

Chapter Four

Highlander Ranch

Caleb shifted in the saddle. "Move them to the left, Blaine!" He motioned with his arm as they moved toward a large rock formation a hundred yards ahead. Seeing Blaine wave, he shifted back, listening for the sounds of any discord within the herd.

He still didn't know why Blaine wanted him to ride point, a position the trail boss usually took if they were short on men. With less than a hundred head, Caleb knew he, Blaine, and the three men from Circle M would have no trouble getting the cattle to the new ranch in a couple hours.

Caleb reined his horse around, watching the three men Ewan and Ian sent. They'd worked at Circle M a couple months before being told they were moving to Settlers Valley. Young and enthusiastic, all worked hard and never complained, no matter the job assigned. The only dissatisfied person was Blaine, who'd hoped for men with more experience.

As he watched, Caleb saw no reason to criticize their work. They drove the cattle well, followed orders, and kept moving with little conversation. He smiled, recalling how the MacLarens never stopped talking when moving the herds at Circle M. Those boys bantered back and forth more than any men he'd ever known.

Reining north, his eyes narrowed on a broad plume of smoke up ahead. Increasing his speed, Caleb rode around a grouping of large boulders, cursing at what he saw. Turning, he nudged Jupiter with his spurs, wasting no time returning to the herd.

"Blaine!" Waving, he rode closer, seeing him turn toward him. "Fire up ahead."

Nodding, Blaine motioned for the three cowhands to circle the herd and hold up before he rode to meet Caleb.

"There's smoke ahead. I think it may be your ranch."

Cursing, Blaine took off, knowing Caleb would follow. Rounding a bend, his heart thudded at the smoke rising from the location of his barn. Racing ahead, he confirmed what he'd suspected. The barn, tool shed, and part of the fence were ablaze.

Slowing enough to jump off Galath, he hurried to the shed, hoping to find a bucket, anything to carry water from the two horse troughs. Reaching the shed, Blaine's hopes sank. Intense heat and rising flames kept him yards away.

Frantic to find a way to stop the fire, he ran back to the barn, ready to go inside, when strong arms banded around him.

"It's too late, Blaine." Caleb pulled him away, continuing the tight hold until he felt the fight go out of him. "There's nothing we can do." Dropping his arms, he took several steps away. "Watch for sparks. We don't want it jumping to the house."

"We've no buckets and only a couple pots." Blaine choked on a plume of smoke. Turning, he hurried up the steps and into the house, grabbing the only items capable of holding water. Taking them outside, he filled one while Caleb filled the other, setting both pots on the ground.

For a long while, neither spoke, both watching for sparks as the barn disintegrated before them.

"At least there weren't any animals in the barn, or much of anything else, as I recall."

Blaine cringed as another beam fell to the ground. He scrubbed a hand down his face. "Aye. But the new tools and some tack were in the shed."

"You can replace those. I'll go into town tomorrow and send a telegram to Ewan."

"Nae. Not until I know what happened." Blaine leveled his gaze at Caleb. "Clear day, little wind, and all the boys were with us. No reason for a fire to start."

"You're thinking someone set it?"

"I'm not sure, lad. All I know is I've seen no reason for it. We hauled all the hay out." He nodded toward the corral next to the barn where the old, rotted hay lay in a big pile. "Took two men half a day to sweep the loft and rake the ground."

"Who would set it? You haven't been here long enough to make enemies."

Blaine stared at the scorched remains of the small structure, shaking his head. "The more we expand our lands, the more enemies the MacLarens make."

"We're not going to solve it right now. Let's finish moving the cattle. By then, we might be able to pick through whatever's left. Might be something worth saving."

Whistling for their horses, they mounted, Caleb turning toward the way they came.

"Hold up a minute, lad. Let's ride around the house, make sure no one's waiting in the back for us to leave."

Blaine rode around one direction, Caleb the other. Meeting up in the back, Blaine motioned for them to continue to the creek on two separate trails. Once there, Blaine slid to the ground, looking for any sign of riders.

"Nothing," Blaine muttered, walking along the bank before returning to his horse. Swinging into the saddle, he reined Galath in a circle before riding to meet Caleb.

"Anything?"

Blaine shook his head. "You're right, lad. Let's get the herd moved and see what we can find after the ashes cool."

Neither pushed their horses as they returned to the herd. First one, then the other would shift to look over their shoulder at the smoldering debris.

"What about those gunmen the other buyers sent out to make counter negotiations on the land?" Caleb asked, unable to get his mind off the unexpected act.

Blaine's brows furrowed. "What do you mean, lad?"

"I'm trying to figure out who would be angry with the MacLarens for buying the land. Changing ownership wouldn't bother the Maidu tribe, and Leland Nettles hasn't expressed an interest in expanding the Acorn Gold Mine this direction. In my mind, that leaves the other buyers wanting to steal it out from under you. Do we know what happened to those three gunmen?"

"Nae. I've heard nothing of them since they left Settlers Valley. We could talk to Nate. I'm still not seeing what good a burned barn would do for them. If they want to drive me out, they'd need to do a lot more than set fire to a couple buildings."

Caleb glanced at him. "They don't know that about you. Of course, it could have been some strange accident or someone who held a grudge against the previous owner."

Blaine continued to watch the trail, wondering if someone might be following them now. "Seems I'm going to be needing extra men sooner than I thought. Once we have the cattle moved and the debris from the fire cleaned up, I'll send a telegram to the uncles, letting them know what happened and that I'm hiring more men."

Rounding the last bend, they spotted the herd and the three cowhands guarding it. Caleb thought of the couple times he'd seen Blaine's frustration when he had to teach them what most ranch hands already knew.

"I understand those boys are young with little experience, but they work hard and learn fast."

Blaine shot a look at Caleb. A little older and a natural leader, he respected his advice. "Aye. I've been a wee hard on them."

"You can be as hard as you want. They just need you to show some patience. The fire doubled the work. I can help some, but—"

"Nae. You've done more than enough for me already, Caleb. You have your own work. Although I wouldn't mind if you helped me look through the ashes. Maybe you'll spot something I'd miss."

"You couldn't keep me away."

Conviction

"You're doing real well, Lia. Are you certain you've never done sutures before?" Hugh Tilden watched over her shoulder as she bandaged the young patient's arm.

She felt heat creep up her face. Lia had never been able to please her father, always falling short of his expectations. Her mother tried to make up for it when her father wasn't around. Still, she'd always felt lacking.

"No, sir. This is the first time. If anyone needed stitching, my mother always did it." A familiar wave of guilt rushed through her before Lia tucked it away, unwilling to spare even a few seconds thinking about what she'd left behind.

"How's he doing, Doc?"

Lia glanced up, startled to see Camden MacLaren stroll into the room. Much like his older brother, Blaine, his tall frame and broad shoulders took up all the extra space.

"Clint's going to be fine." Hugh shot a firm gaze at the ten-year-old. "I'd advise you and Banner learn to settle your differences without tossing one another out of the barn."

The young boy's eyes moved to his cousin, Camden. Seeing his stern expression, Clint nodded. "Yes, sir."

"I know he's your twin and you're going to fight once in a while. Just don't make it a habit."

"Yeah, I know. But Banner shouldn't have left the rack for me to trip over."

"Clint..." Camden stepped next to the table.

"He did it on purpose, Cam."

Shaking his head, Camden leaned down to whisper into his cousin's ear. "You're a MacLaren, lad, and I expect you to act like it. We'll speak of this at home."

Pursing his lips, Clint nodded.

Camden straightened. "Can I take him back to the ranch now?"

Hugh nodded. "Keep the arm clean and don't get it wet for at least a week. Bring him back to the clinic in two weeks and we'll take out the sutures. Now, tell me when Sean is scheduled to leave for Scotland."

Camden saw the dejected look on Clint's face at the mention of Sean. Even if it was what he wanted, everyone felt the same about him leaving for veterinary school.

"The lad leaves in a few weeks. Ma and the aunts are planning a shindig. We'll let you know when." Camden turned his attention to Lia. "You, too. We're hoping the family in Settlers Valley will be able to ride to town for it. I'm sure at least one of them would be glad to see you."

Hugh sent a questioning look at her as heat crawled up Lia's neck and onto her face.

"I'll see, Cam. Between my jobs at the Gold Dust and here, I'm not sure there'll be time."

"I'm sure Joe and I can figure something out, Lia," Hugh offered. "If I go, my wife and children will be coming with me. You can ride in the wagon with us."

Her mind spinning at the thought of seeing Blaine again, she nodded. "Thank you."

"All right, Clint. Let's get you over to see your big brother before we leave town."

He slid off the table to the floor. "Ah, Cam. Do we have to see Brodie? He'll just get mad at me and Banner for fighting."

"Aye, lad, he might. It's time to get it over with." Camden motioned for him to move toward the door. "Thanks, Doc." Smiling at Lia, he stepped next to her. "If you have an interest, lass, you might want to send Blaine a letter. Send it to him at the post office. Nate will make sure he gets it."

"I don't know, Cam. He, well...Blaine and I hardly know each other."

"Isn't that why you would be writing him, lass?" Grinning, he turned toward the door. "Think on it."

Clutching her hands in front of her, Lia watched as Camden and Clint left, feeling an odd sense of excitement. She'd never thought of writing Blaine.

"I think it might be a good idea, Lia."

Her brows knit in confusion. "What might be?"

Hugh leaned against the table, crossing his arms. "Writing Blaine."

Eyes widening, she shook her head. "I don't know, Doctor. We hardly know each other. I'm sure he doesn't even remember me."

Chuckling, Hugh pushed away from the table. "Oh, I'm sure he remembers you, Lia. As Cam said, it's up to you." Grabbing his coat from a hook, he moved next to her. "If you're finished, I'll walk you to the Gold Dust."

"You don't need to do that. It isn't far."

He looked out the front windows. "It's getting dark, and the hotel is on my way home."

Slipping into her coat, Lia walked out ahead of him, her body stilling at the sight of two riders. Heart pounding, she turned away from them, increasing her pace along the boardwalk.

"Is everything all right, Lia?" Hugh shifted, seeking anything that may have frightened her.

Refusing to turn around, she walked faster. "I forgot Joe wanted me there a little early today."

"I'm sure he'll forgive a few minutes."

Reaching the front door of the Gold Dust, Lia shifted enough to see Hugh's face. "Thank you, Doctor. Please give my regards to your wife."

"I'll do that. Have a pleasant night and I'll see you tomorrow."

She slipped inside, closing the door and taking a deep breath. Her heart continued to pound at a rapid rate. Whirling around, Lia peered out the front window. The riders were nowhere in sight.

"Maybe I imagined seeing them," she murmured, placing a hand on her chest.

"Lia, are you ready to get to work?"

She hadn't noticed Joe walk up. At his concerned expression, she swallowed the panic and nodded.

"Let me put my coat away and I'll join you in the kitchen."

He studied her face, giving a curt nod before walking away. Grateful he didn't ask more questions, she hurried to her room in the back. Closing the door, Lia forced herself to take a deep breath, doing her best to forget the two riders. Rubbing her eyes, she took the apron from its hook, returning to the front as she tied it around her waist.

Joe didn't look up from where he cut vegetables at the table. "Put the bread in the oven, would you, girl? And make sure the pies are cooling on the rack."

"Sure." These were jobs she did almost every day in preparation for the supper crowd. Lia didn't need to think about them, just make sure everything was the way Joe wanted it.

Placing the first loaf into the oven, she stepped back, thinking of the two men. Their build and horses were so much like she remembered. It had been years, but some things didn't change.

"But, Brodie, it wasn't my fault this time." Clint sat in a chair across from his oldest brother. *Why did he have to be the sheriff?* he thought, waiting to hear his punishment.

"It's never one person's fault, Clint. If Da had been home and not in Sacramento, he'd come down pretty hard on you, lad." Brodie leaned forward, resting his arms on the desk. "What do you think is a suitable punishment for disobeying Da?"

Gripping the arms of the chair, Clint shook his head. "I don't know."

"What do you think, Cam? Helping the aunts with supper for a week?"

Clint shot from his chair. "That's not right, Brodie. Da wouldn't do that."

"I'm thinking Uncle Ewan would do something real close, Clint."

The boy swiveled toward Camden. "He'd have me milk the cows or tend the pigs, not work inside with the women." His nose wrinkled at the thought. "I'm not a girl."

"At ten, you and Banner are almost men. But you can't stop fighting."

Crossing his arms, Clint sat down. "You and Colin used to fight. And Quinn, too."

Brodie worked to keep the smile off his face. "Aye. And we all got punished for it, too."

"What did Da make you do?"

Rubbing his chin, Brodie looked up at the ceiling as he tried to remember. "Ach. Once, he made us muck the entire barn for a month."

Clint's face twisted into a scowl.

"Another time, we had to gather eggs and clean the chicken coop."

Sitting back in the chair, Clint's shoulders slumped.

"And remember the time Uncle Ewan ordered you to take care of Clint and Banner?" Camden leaned against the desk, smirking at the worst punishment any boy could imagine. "They weren't even a year old. You had to change their clothes, bathe them, make their food and get it down their throats. Funniest thing I ever saw." He chuckled at the memory.

Brodie shook his head. "Worst week of my life."

"Me and Banner can't do that, Brodie. We don't have any babies at the ranch."

He cast a quick look at Camden. "I suppose Maggie could move to the ranch with Shaun for a week. It'd help you lads to get to know your cousin."

Eyes wide with horror, Clint crossed his arms. "Or—"

Before Brodie could finish, the door burst open. Two men walked inside, both in black from their hats to their boots. Both with long beards—one almost white, the other black, sprinkled with flecks of silver. The older man stepped forward.

"Are you the sheriff?"

Brodie stood, walking around the desk. "Aye. I'm Brodie MacLaren. Can I help you?"

The man stared him up and down before taking the hand Brodie offered. "I'm Porter Jacobs and this is my son, Orson. We've come from Salt Lake City."

"Are you looking to settle here in Conviction, Mr. Porter?"

The older man scowled. "Absolutely not. We're looking for a runaway and we think she's living here. She's my daughter."

Brodie glanced at Clint, seeing his brother's eyes grow wide. "I'll do what I can. When did she run away?"

"Almost four years ago."

"Four years is a long time. How old was she, Mr. Jacobs?"

Porter glanced away, appearing to count the years. "Seventeen. She left a week before her marriage. She'd be twenty now. Almost too old for a third wife, but her betrothed is a generous man and has decided to wait for her return."

Brodie's brows rose at his words.

Orson stepped forward, casting a look between his father and Brodie. "He's an elder in the church. My sister should be proud to be selected by him."

"Instead, she slipped away in the darkness of night, leaving her family." Porter spat out the words, his face twisting. Reaching into his pocket, he pulled out an old, yellowed photograph, wrinkled from use. "This was taken when she was twelve."

Brodie took it from the man's hand, studying it, a knot forming in his stomach. "The lass doesn't look like anyone from around here, Mr. Jacobs."

"She's much older now."

Brodie sighed. He was tired, wanted to settle the punishment for Clint and Banner, and get home to Maggie. "As I said, I'll do what I can." Glancing at the photograph once more, his throat tightened, dreading the answer to the question he had to ask. "What's your daughter's name?"

"Her name is Permilia. Permilia Jacobs."

Chapter Five

Camden's eyes widened before he caught a warning look from Brodie and an almost imperceptible nod at the door.

"I've a quick errand to run." Camden looked at his cousin. "Clint, come with me. We'll stop back before riding to the ranch."

Ready to get away from his brother and the decision on punishment, Clint jumped out of the chair. Moving around Porter and Orson, he risked a quick glance at the older man, shrinking away at the hostility on his face. Yanking the door open, he dashed outside, Camden right behind him.

"I don't like those men, Cam."

"I cannot dispute that, lad. Come on. It's urgent I go speak with someone."

Being careful to avoid the wagons and cowboys as they crossed the wide dirt street, Camden headed up the street, opening the door to the Gold Dust.

"Do we get to eat here tonight?" The excitement in Clint's voice matched the smile on his face.

"Nae. Not tonight, lad. Sit over there." He pointed to a group of chairs. "I'll be back in a minute."

Deflating, Clint dragged his feet to the chair, sitting down to watch the activity in the dining room. He tracked Camden's movements as he walked toward a nice looking lady talking to a group of people around a table. When she stepped away, Camden leaned down to whisper into her ear. A moment later, they moved out of Clint's view.

Lia stopped next to the kitchen door, turning to look up. "Do you need a table, Cam?" The warmth she'd become accustomed to seeing on his face had disappeared.

"Not tonight, lass." He took a quick look behind him before returning his attention to her. "Do you know Porter and Orson Jacobs?"

Her startled expression, terror in her eyes, gave him the answer. "I..." Lia clamped her mouth shut, her gaze darting behind him.

Looking down, he saw her clutch both hands so hard, the knuckles turned white. "Is Porter your father?"

Closing her eyes, she nodded.

"And Orson is your brother."

When she opened them, his gut clenched at the stark fear on her face. "Yes. He's the oldest boy." Reaching behind her, Lia untied the apron, wadding it in her hand. "I have to get out of here."

He grabbed her arm as she started to turn away. "Not yet. Brodie is stalling them." Camden glanced behind him once more. "They have an old photograph of you. I didn't see it, so I don't know if you still look the same. Go to your room and stay there until either Brodie or I come for you. I'll talk to Joe. It's good he has others to help in the dining room tonight."

Shaking her head, she tried to pull her arm away, stopping when his grip tightened. "This is the best hotel in town, Cam. I won't be able to stay in my room for days."

"Then come back to the ranch with me and Clint. We've plenty of room, and they'll never find you way out there."

Sucking in a shaky breath, she did her best to calm the thudding in her chest. "This isn't your problem, Cam."

"Nae, lass. You're a friend, and a special friend to Blaine. He'd be telling you the same if he hadn't left town. Pack what you have and meet us out back. I'll speak with Joe." Dropping his hold on her arm, he turned away.

"Cam?"

Stopping, he glanced over his shoulder. "Aye?"

"Thank you."

Circle M

"I'm sorry for the inconvenience, Mrs. MacLaren."

Camden's mother, Kyla, touched Lia's arm. "Ach. You're no trouble at all. Cam did the right thing, bringing you to us. Follow me upstairs and I'll show you where you'll be staying." Reaching the second floor, she continued down the hall to the last room. "This is Blaine's room. He'll not be here for a while."

Stepping into the room behind Kyla, she looked around, her mouth going dry at the knowledge she'd be sleeping in Blaine's bed. "It's very nice."

"Aye, it is. He's a neat lad, always putting everything in its place." Kyla nodded toward a wall where a single picture hung. "That's a photograph of the family before Angus was murdered. Colin, Blaine, and Camden each have one. They cost us a pretty penny back then, but I'm, um...thankful we have them." She turned away, her voice breaking on the last.

"I heard of your husband's death. I'm so sorry."

Jaw tightening, Kyla nodded. "My husband, Angus, and Quinn's da, Gillis, were murdered the same day. But we'll not be talking of it more today. Have you had supper?"

"No, ma'am."

"Please, call me Kyla. I kept food warm for Camden, and there's plenty, so you can eat supper with him. Don't be surprised if my two youngest, Chrissy and Alana, sit at the table with you. They love having company."

Setting her satchel on the bed, Lia followed Kyla into the hall. "What can I do to help?"

"You could find Camden, lass. I think he's out in the barn with the lads. It will take me no time to fill the plates." Kyla hastened to the kitchen while Lia stepped outside.

Closing the door, she studied the sprawling area where the MacLarens lived. Even in the growing darkness, she could see four large houses in a long row spaced about a hundred yards apart. Across from each house stood a barn, Kyla's being the largest. Children, ranging from four or five to eleven or twelve, ran around or chatted in small groups. She remembered Blaine once telling her his mother and aunts took turns schooling the youngest. Depending on the weather, the older children rode to the schoolhouse in town, hurrying back to complete chores before supper.

The scene reminded her somewhat of home, except the houses were smaller and there were few horses. The Jacobs family were farmers, not ranchers, toiling in the dirt instead of breeding and raising cattle.

"What do you think?" Blaine's older brother, Colin, walked up the porch steps, stopping next to her.

"It's lovely. I've never seen another ranch as large. I'm certain it takes a great deal of work to manage."

Crossing his arms, he leaned against a post. "Aye, it does. From what I've heard, the house Blaine lives in is about the same size as ours."

She bit her lip. "You haven't seen it?"

"Nae. I'll ride up after we drive the herd to market this year. Sarah may ride along in the wagon with Grant. She wants to visit her sister, Geneen. We're hoping to be there before Heather has her wee bairn."

"She's expecting?"

A stunning smile, so much like Blaine's, flashed across Colin's face. "Aye. The lass thinks the bairn will come in July." He looked at her, his expression sobering. "Thank you for what you did for Maggie. Brodie would've lost his mind if he'd lost her."

She shook her head, feeling her cheeks flush. "People are giving me too much praise for the little I did. The doctors are the ones who helped her. All I did was hold Maggie's hand and talk to her."

"Whatever you did, lass, it helped. Even Maggie says as much."

"Have you found Camden?"

Both shifted to see Kyla standing behind them. Lia's eyes widened.

"I'm so sorry. I got to talking and forgot." She hurried down the steps. "I'll get him now," she called over her shoulder.

"Such a nice lass, don't you think, Colin?"

A grin tipped up the corners of his mouth. "Aye, Ma, I do."

"Is she the one Blaine rode out to see right after the ceremony for Geneen and Nate?"

"Aye, Ma, she is."

Kyla stayed next to Colin, watching Lia and Camden emerge from the barn, laughing at something.

"Could be trouble if the lass stays around here too long."

His mother's meaning wasn't lost on Colin. "Nae, Ma. Cam won't be trying to steal what belongs to Blaine."

"So it's like that, is it?"

Chuckling, Colin nodded. "Aye, Ma. I'm afraid it is. For both Blaine and Lia. They just haven't had the time to figure it out."

"I found him." Lia climbed the steps, unaware of the smirks as she walked past Kyla and Colin. "Being so tall, I doubt you ever have trouble finding him."

"The lad is the giant among us, lass." Colin clasped his brother on the shoulder. "I'm heading down to Quinn's, Ma. I think Sarah is down there with Emma. It's good to see you, Lia."

"You, too, Colin."

"Well, don't stand there, you two. Supper is waiting on the table and I'm not heating it up again."

"Thank you for inviting me out here, Cam."

He stepped aside to let her precede him into the house. "Did your da mean what he said about you running away before your marriage?" Walking into the dining room, he pulled out a chair for her.

Sitting down, Lia looked at the full plate, wondering if she should tell him the truth or not. She'd never been good at lying.

"I suppose that's accurate, at least from my father's viewpoint."

Sitting next to her, he picked up his fork. "Seems you were to be married or not, lass. Which was it?"

Spearing a piece of roast, he put it into his mouth and chewed, noticing her fidgeting beside him.

Pushing the food around her plate, Lia let out a shaky breath. "Where I come from, it's normal for a father to select who his daughters marry. The man my father chose for me was older with two other wives." Biting her bottom lip, she continued to stare at her food.

Cam remembered what Porter had told Brodie. He tried to keep his voice even. "I've only heard of such a thing. Never met anybody with more than one."

"It's quite common where I lived, although the government is trying to stop it. Some men have been taken to jail for practicing polygamy. It never bothered my father, though. He has four wives, my mother being his first. His fourth wife was younger than me." She glanced at him, trying to hide her discomfort. "It made me sick to see him usher her into his bedroom at night."

"What about your ma?"

Setting her fork down, she drew in a breath. "She loved my father. When he took a second wife, she accepted it. I was too young to understand. He took his third wife when I was twelve. She was sixteen. That's when I saw a real change in my mother. When he married his fourth, Mother came to me and suggested I consider leaving. She didn't want me to go through the same pain as her. Mother helped me plan my escape." A grim smile crossed her face as she looked at Camden. "That's what she called it. One night, when Father took his fourth wife into his room and locked the door, she came to me, saying it was time. I grabbed the satchel we'd left hidden in the barn, saddled an old horse, and left."

Camden had stopped eating halfway through her story, fascinated by what she had to accept and how strong she had to have been to leave alone. "You were quite brave, lass. Many women would've accepted it, lived with what they'd been given."

Shaking her head, a deep sadness washed over her. "I have no family." Her tired gaze met his. "Father doesn't want to take me back to marry. He wants me back to publicly shame me as punishment for embarrassing him and the man he intended I marry."

A slow anger grew within him. He couldn't imagine any father behaving in such a cruel way to their own daughter. "Then what would happen?"

Lia shrugged. "I don't know. He'd probably force me to marry a man even older than his friend." A sudden wave of panic overtook her. "You won't tell anyone, will you, Cam?"

Leaning his arms against the edge of the table, he studied her face. "I cannot promise you that, lass." Seeing a flash of pain cross her face, he continued. "Brodie will need to know, as will Ma and maybe some others. We can decide who once we know how long your da and brother will be staying in town."

"I can't stay here for long, Cam. Joe won't hold my job for long. Not with so many people looking for work."

"You'll stay here as long as it takes, lass. Blaine wouldn't want it any other way."

She shot a hard look at him. "How do you know what Blaine would want?"

Chuckling, he pushed his empty plate away. "We're brothers."

"I know that. It still doesn't explain why you think he'd care about anything I do."

"Blaine cares. I've never seen him look at any lass the way he looks at you. It's too bad the uncles sent him to Settlers Valley when they did. As much as he needed to get away, I'm thinking he would've rather stayed here to be around you."

"Did his needing to leave have anything to do with what happened around Christmas?"

"Aye. It did."

Leaning forward, she locked her gaze with Camden's. "Can you tell me what happened?"

Sliding back his chair, he stood. "It's Blaine's story to tell, lass. I've got a few more chores to do before turning in. Let's get these dishes done." He stepped behind her, pulling out the chair.

"You go ahead and finish your work, Cam. I can get these done in a few minutes."

"If you're sure."

"I am."

Picking up the plates, Lia walked into the kitchen, grateful for a few minutes alone to consider what to do next.

It had been close to four years since she'd left Salt Lake City and her family's farm. Each day had been a struggle to earn enough for food and lodging. Her clothes were so frayed, Lia often felt embarrassed to be seen in them.

She'd almost given up during her stay in Sacramento. Her job in a restaurant, similar to the Gold Dust, ended when she refused the advances of her boss. With no money and few prospects, Lia had made the difficult decision to return home.

Packing her belongings, she'd trudged to the stagecoach station, stopping to speak with a customer she used to serve. Their brief conversation brought new hope. The steamship captain offered to take her to his next stop up the Feather River in return for serving drinks to the passengers. She'd accepted with eager anticipation.

The steamer left the following morning. When it docked, the captain slipped her an extra dollar, recommending she talk to Joe at the Gold Dust. Not stopping along the way, she walked into the restaurant, head high and back straight. He'd hired her within seconds of hearing the captain's name, handed her an apron, and pointed to the dining room.

Her life turned around and improved with each passing week. She worked hard and even splurged for a new cotton dress. Then Joe had spoken to the doctors. She'd gone to bed each night sending up thanks for the second chance, falling asleep to the image of a tall cowboy with broad shoulders, dark hair, and an infectious smile. Seeing him again would make all her dreams a reality.

After drying the last plate, she trudged up the stairs to the end of the hall. An odd excitement overcame her when she opened the bedroom door. Stepping inside, the first item she spotted was her satchel sitting on Blaine's bed. The knowledge he'd slept in the same bed she'd be using rippled through her, creating an unexpected warmth.

Changing clothes, she slipped under the sheets, drawing the coverlet under her chin. The arrival of her father and brother changed everything. She had no idea how they'd found her and couldn't stay around to find out. It wouldn't take long for them to come across someone who paired their description of a runaway daughter with her.

As much as Lia appreciated help from the MacLarens, she couldn't impose on their generosity. She'd taken care of herself too long to be in anyone's debt. Especially the most powerful family in the region.

Glancing across the room at her open satchel, Lia let out a weary breath. Everything of value she owned was inside. She could leave at any time, except for one small issue. No transportation.

Staring at the ceiling, an idea began to form. It wouldn't be easy and would include a good deal of risk. If she could just get back to town...

Chapter Six

"Do you have any proof the fire was intentional?" Nate blew across the top of his cup, taking a sip of coffee.

Rubbing his neck, Blaine paced to the window of the jail, noting the riders on the street. It was eight o'clock in the morning. He should be at his ranch, helping the men rebuild the barn. Instead, he'd ridden to town to see Nate and try to figure out what to do next.

"Nothing except a gut feeling. Caleb and I searched around the barn, the house, and north to the creek. We didn't find anything."

"And the barn had been cleaned out."

Blaine nodded. "The ranch hands and I finished it two days before the fire. There was nothing inside or against the outside that would start a fire. We got rid of every scrap of brush around the walls." Blaine lowered himself into a chair opposite Nate. "Caleb thinks it's someone who has a grudge against me."

"Or your family. The MacLarens are successful and continue to increase their holdings. Jealousy can be a powerful incentive."

"Aye. I've thought of that. If that's true, it means the same people could come after Heather and Geneen."

Nate set his cup down, mumbling an oath. "Any idea who it could be?"

"Caleb thinks it might be those boys who tried to buy the land before we closed the sale."

A fierce expression twisted his face. "When we booted them out of town, I told them to never come back or they'd regret it."

Blaine shrugged. "Could be they didn't listen to you, lad."

"And it could be they left and never returned."

Standing, Blaine rested a hand on the desk, leaning forward. "Aye, it's possible. My gut tells me otherwise, Nate."

"And I respect your gut, but there's no proof the fire was intentional." Pushing up, he walked around the desk. "You'll need more men to guard the ranch."

Blaine turned around, crossing his arms. "And where do you suggest I find these men, lad?"

He let out an exasperated breath. "Hell if I know. I've posted that you're hiring. So far, I've gotten an old man too bent over to work in the mine and a ten-year-old boy who wants to get away from his pa." Nate rubbed his brow. "I've met the man and don't blame the boy. Anyway, I suppose I could ride to the Acorn and ask Nettles to spread the word."

"The man's a scoundrel," Blaine scoffed.

"True, but he may know of men who'd rather work a ranch than in a mine. Has Caleb mentioned hiring extra help?"

"Nae. We both know the lad can't afford them. After I leave here, I'm sending a telegram to Ewan and Ian to let them know what happened. I need their help finding hands for both ranches. They won't ignore any threat to Heather and Geneen."

Watching as Blaine walked toward the door, Nate stepped in front of him. "Caleb is stubborn. Don't be surprised if he refuses help."

"Aye, I've thought of that. I also know the lad will do everything he can to protect Heather and Geneen."

Nate moved aside, studying his friend's face. "You really do believe the fire was intentional."

Blaine opened the door, stepping outside onto the boardwalk. Glancing behind him, he nodded at Nate. "Aye. I believe it was no accident."

Blaine sauntered toward the telegraph office, his pace slow and deliberate, looking at the face of every cowboy who rode or walked past. He tried convincing himself the fire had been an accident. Each time, he shoved the thought aside.

If it had burned the bunkhouse, there would have been reason to believe the men failed to extinguish the smoldering embers in the cook stove or the one at the other end used for additional heat in the winter. The fire was nowhere near the building where his men ate and slept.

Reaching the telegraph office, he stopped, watching a group of three riders approach from the south. Stepping to the edge of the boardwalk, Blaine studied their faces, the way they rode, their expressions. All wore gunbelts strapped around their waists, their gazes moving in slow assessment of the small town.

He didn't recognize them, but believed they were either cowhands or gunmen. Stopping in front of the Lucky Lady, the larger of the two saloons in Settlers Valley, he waited until they dismounted and walked inside.

Blaine wanted to follow them, but needed to get a message off to Brodie and another to his uncles. He stepped into the telegraph office and finished his business before heading straight for the saloon.

The three sat at a table near the window, nursing their drinks and talking. Taking a spot at the bar, he waved off Benji, the owner of the Lucky Lady, when he offered a whiskey.

"A wee bit early for me."

Leaning his muscled arms on the bar, Benji raised a brow. "What brings you in here, Blaine?"

"Someone burned down my barn."

Benji let out a breath. "You sure it wasn't an accident?"

Explaining the same reasons he gave Nate, Blaine shot another look at the three men. "I'm in here to spread the word I need more men."

Benji followed his gaze. "I don't know anything about those three over there. This is their first time in the saloon."

"Guess I'd best go introduce myself."

Walking up to them, he waited until they stopped talking and looked at him. "Are you lads passing through or looking for work?"

The oldest sat back. "Who's asking?"

Blaine held out his hand. "I'm Blaine MacLaren. I own a ranch east of here and need more men."

Standing, the man grasped the outstretched hand. "I'm Cal Dempsey. These are my brothers, Newt and Will. You said something about jobs?" Cal motioned to an empty chair.

Sitting down, Blaine leaned back. "I've got three cowhands already. I need at least three more. Are you lads looking to stay around a while?"

Cal looked at his brothers, shrugging. "We need work. I'm not sure how long we'll be staying."

"Do you have any experience on a ranch?"

"Been working at ranches the last two years. Ever since we left the 19th Indiana Infantry."

Blaine's gaze narrowed. "All three of you fought for the Union?"

Cal nodded. "We did. Got out in early 1864 and decided to ride west. Found work in Kansas, then New Mexico. Newt has been wanting to see the Pacific Ocean, so we decided to travel this way."

Blaine looked at Newt. "Did you see the ocean, lad?"

The corners of Newt's mouth slid upwards. "Sure did. Quite a sight."

"We darn near ran out of money in San Francisco." Will leaned back, crossing his arms. "Heard about the

Acorn Mine up this way and decided we'd see if they are hiring."

"If that's what you want to do, Leland Nettles is always hiring."

Cal picked up his drink, taking a sip. "Sounds like you don't like the man, MacLaren."

Blaine winced, thinking he'd been able to hide his disdain for Nettles. "I've not had the chance to deal much with him. If you want to learn more, I'd suggest you talk to Benji behind the bar or Marcus Kamm, the owner of the blacksmith and livery." The chair scraped against the wood floor as he stood. "If you lads decide you'd rather work for a brand than a mine, you can get a message to me through the sheriff, Nate Hollis." Shaking each of their hands, he nodded at Benji before leaving for the livery.

"Blaine!"

Swinging around, he waited for Josiah Lloyd to catch up to him.

"Already got a return telegram from the sheriff in Conviction." Holding it out to Blaine, he sucked in a deep breath. "Do you want me to wait for a reply?"

Reading through the short message, Blaine shook his head. "Nae. I've what I need. Thanks, Josiah."

"Anytime. Well, guess I'd best get back to the office. The stage will be coming through anytime."

Turning, Blaine felt a rush of relief. Brodie knew of two ranch hands looking for work in a smaller town.

They planned to leave Conviction that afternoon and would talk to Nate.

Stepping into the street, he looked up at the sky. "Thank you, Brodie," he murmured, changing directions to head to the jail. Pushing the door open, he held up the message as he stepped inside. "Brodie's sending two lads this way. He told them to talk to you when they got to town." Closing the door, he sat down.

"Excellent news. If you can find two or three more, you'll have enough men for your ranch and Caleb's."

The door burst open, a man Nate didn't recognize stepping inside. "What can I do for you?"

"I'm looking for..." His voice trailed off when his gaze landed on Blaine. "Mr. MacLaren?"

Looking over his shoulder, Blaine stood. "Mr. Dempsey."

"Is your offer still open?"

Keeping his expression neutral, he nodded. "Aye, it is."

Taking off his hat, Cal fingered the brim. "My brothers and me, well, we'd be interested in taking those jobs."

Offering his hand, the corners of Blaine's mouth tilted up. "That's good news. Be ready in ten minutes and I'll take you there."

Shaking his hand, Cal smiled. "Thank you, Mr. MacLaren."

"It's Blaine, and you can thank me after you see how much work you'll be doing."

"Hard work never bothered us before, and it won't bother us now. I'll get Newt and Will. We'll meet you..."

"At the livery, lad."

Nodding at Nate, Cal closed the door behind him.

A broad grin crossed Nate's face. "Three more, huh?"

"Brothers who rode into town today. They've some experience. When the two Brodie sends get here, send them to Caleb. I'll stop by there on the way home and let him know."

"Have you heard from Ewan and Ian about paying their wages?"

Blaine shook his head. "Not yet, but I'm not worried. They'll not let anything happen to Heather and Geneen, and they want Caleb to succeed. The lad has already spent more time at my place than he should."

Nate stood, placing his hand on the desk and leaning forward. "You keep calling it your place, not Circle M. I think you need to come up with a name for your ranch."

Chuckling, Blaine crossed his arms. "It's not my ranch. It belongs to the family."

"It does, but I think it should have its own name." Straightening, Nate walked around the desk, resting a hip against the edge. "I'm thinking you, Caleb, and I ought to have a meeting to decide what to call it."

A wry grin appeared on his face. "All right, laddie. It's Thursday. Bring the lasses and come to my place Sunday for supper, and—"

Nate snorted, holding up a hand. "Oh, hell no. You come to Highlander Ranch. The ladies will cook and we'll talk."

Blaine's grin faded. "You don't like my cooking?"

"All I'll say is we'll be in a better mood to discuss naming the ranch if Geneen and Heather make the meal. Be there by noon."

Touching the brim of his hat, Blaine nodded. "Noon it is."

Circle M

"I need to return to town, Cam. It's been several days and I need to work." Lia tossed her few possessions into her satchel.

Camden stood in the doorway, his shoulder resting against the frame. "Brodie says your da and brother are still in town. What if they see you?"

Staring down, she shoved aside the dread at the thought of them seeing her. "I know it's a risk."

"They're staying at the Gold Dust, Lia. You'll not be able to avoid them."

"I can't stay here forever, Cam. You and your family have been wonderful, but I need to take care of this on my own."

Crossing his arms, he studied her. "And how do you propose to do that?"

Turning toward him, she lifted her chin. "Find someone to help me get away."

Nostrils flaring, his jaw tightened. "If you want to leave, I'll take you some place safe. We'll let Joe know, then be off."

"Absolutely not. I've seen how much work you do around here, how much your family needs every available person." She bit her lip, a bleak expression on her face. "I've been thinking of leaving for a while now, Cam." The lie rolled out of her mouth easier than she'd imagined.

Pushing away from the door, he walked toward her. "You're lying to me, lass."

Crossing her arms, Lia glared at him. "I am not. This has been the longest I've stayed anywhere since leaving home. It's time I moved on."

"What of your work at the clinic? The doctors will be missing you if you leave."

A bleak expression crossed her face. "I know, but leaving is for the best."

"And what of Blaine?"

Her mouth fell open before she snapped it closed. Squaring her shoulders, Lia met his gaze. "What does Blaine have to do with this?"

A cocky grin lifted one corner of his mouth. "Are you saying you have no feelings for the lad?"

A slow sadness slipped through her at the thought of Blaine. "He left, Cam. Whether I have feelings for him or not doesn't matter any longer."

The cockiness disappeared at the sorrow in her voice. "The lad won't be up there forever, Lia."

"Perhaps not, but by the time he returns, I doubt he'll remember me. I mean, they *do* have women in Settlers Valley, don't they?"

An amused grin tipped the corners of his mouth. "I'm sure they do, lass. It doesn't mean Blaine would show an interest in them."

"And it doesn't mean he won't." She sucked in a shaky breath, looking at her meager possessions. "I appreciate what you're trying to say, Cam. The truth is I like Blaine very much. The reality is he's gone and may not come back. I have to think of myself right now, and going back to work—" She stopped at the sound of boots pounding up the stairs.

"Cam, Lia, are you two up here?"

Camden walked to the open doorway. "In here, Brodie. I didn't know you were coming today."

"Maggie wanted to bring Shaun to the ranch for a visit. We'll be staying overnight so we can be here for Sunday supper." He looked at Lia. "I've news of your family, lass."

"Did they find out I'm here?" Her voice shook, body growing tense.

"Nae. It's good news. Your da came by the jail this morning. Someone told them a lass who fit your description left for Martinez a few weeks ago. They've decided to leave tomorrow."

Shoulders sagging, she sat on the edge of the bed. "They're leaving?"

Brodie nodded. "Aye. Tomorrow, lass. If you want, you can ride back to town with us tomorrow after supper."

"You're sure they're leaving?" A knot formed in her stomach, warning Lia not to put too much trust in what her father told Brodie.

"Aye. Your da is convinced you were here but moved on. From the way he acted, it's doubtful the two of them will return."

Blowing out a breath, she allowed herself the slightest amount of hope Brodie was right. Standing, she walked up to him.

"You've brought wonderful news. I can't thank you or your family enough for all you've done." She looked between the two men, moisture building in her eyes.

"Ah, lass. This calls for a celebration, not tears." Camden offered his arm. "I'll escort you downstairs to visit with Maggie and Shaun. You've been given a new start, Lia."

Slipping her arm through his, she smiled. "Yes, I certainly have."

Even as she said the words, something inside her curled into a ball of worry. If she understood anything about her family, it was they rarely took the word of one person before making a decision.

Walking down the stairs, Camden at her side, she spotted Kyla cradling Shaun in her arms. The sight forced Lia to shove her uneasiness aside. Her father and brother were gone. She was free to return to town, continuing her work for Joe and at the clinic.

Camden was right. Tonight, she'd celebrate another chance, not fret over silly, unfounded fears.

Chapter Seven

Conviction

"It's good to have you back, girl." Joe wiped his hands down his apron, motioning for Lia to put hers on before he grabbed a pot, setting it on the counter. "With it being Monday morning and no steamship docking, it shouldn't be too busy. I'm sure the doctors will be glad to see you."

"Unless you need me here, I'm planning to work there this afternoon."

"I'm sure they'd appreciate it. From what I heard, there was a fight at Buckie's Castle Friday night. Vickery and Tilden were up most of the night patching up broken bones and cut faces. Gwen came by here and said Brodie put several of them in jail until Saturday afternoon." Joe placed his hands on his hips and chuckled. "It's never dull around this town anymore."

Her eyes crinkled at the corners, remembering Brodie telling the same story Sunday at supper. Two of his deputies, Seth Montero and Alex Campbell, spent Friday night at the jail trying to keep the nine prisoners from throwing more punches.

"You're awful quiet this morning." He stopped slicing potatoes to look at her. "Something bothering you?"

"No, Joe. I'm fine." Shifting from one foot to the other, she glanced at him. "I guess Cam or Brodie told you why I had to leave town for a few days."

"Yep. They were right to get you away."

She bit her lip, deciding whether to ask the question burning inside her. "Brodie told me my father and brother were staying here. Did they ask you about me?"

Setting down the knife, he straightened. "They described a woman who could've been any of a hundred ladies in this town. The photograph they showed me was old and not much help."

When he stopped, she stared at him, waiting for more.

"I told them the truth. The photograph didn't remind me of any woman I'd ever seen." He shot her a conspiratorial grin, lifting his brows. "The last I heard, they'd ridden west to Martinez. I doubt they'll be back this way."

The same knot that twisted her stomach at Brodie's announcement on Saturday began to take hold again. Most of the MacLarens agreed with Joe and Brodie about her father and brother not returning. Lia wished she felt as certain.

"I hope you're right."

A sound from the front had her turning toward the dining room. "I believe the first customers of the morning have arrived. Are you ready?"

Joe tossed bacon fat into a large cast iron skillet, lifting a brow as he glanced over his shoulder. "Girl, this kitchen is always ready."

Hiding a smile, Lia touched a hand to her hair before walking into the front. Stopping to gaze around the room, her heart faltered. Her father and brother sat at a table near the window, their backs to her.

Spinning around, she untied her apron, holding it in a tight grip as she ran down the hall to her room. Lia's panicked gaze swept around the space. The satchel sat on a chair, still packed with the possessions she'd taken to the MacLarens.

Lifting the mattress, she reached underneath, pulling out the pouch holding all the money she'd stashed away. For most, it didn't amount to much. For Lia, it meant the difference between being discovered and living free.

Slipping the pouch into the pocket of her dress, she stuffed the last of her belongings into the satchel before latching it. She had to leave town right away. Lia placed a hand against her forehead, forcing herself to think.

The stage didn't pass through Conviction on Monday, and Joe had already said there'd be no steamship docking. Lia didn't own a horse or buggy, and the closest town was days away by foot. Staring at the door leading to the alley behind the restaurant, she hesitated, not knowing where to go or who to ask for help.

Lia had but one ally in town, and she hesitated to burden him with another request. Joe had already done more for her than anyone since she'd left home. Still...

Making a hasty decision, she grabbed the satchel, slipped outside, and ran around to the door of the kitchen. Peeking through the dust-covered windows, Lia spotted her boss at the stove, brandishing a spatula. Looking toward the opening between the kitchen and dining room, she turned the knob on the back door.

"Joe?"

He whipped around, causing bits of food on the spatula to fly through the air. "Where in tarnation have you been? The other server is going mad working all the tables."

Her face flushed in misery, she took a step toward him. "My father and brother are in the dining room. I have to get away."

His anger vanishing, Joe set down the spatula and walked to her, placing a comforting hand on her shoulder. "Then we'll find a way to do it. Sit over there, in the corner by the closet while I finish up. When all the customers are gone, you and I will figure something out."

"Where are we going?" Lia followed Joe along the alley behind the Gold Dust. She rarely walked the narrow passage, preferring the main street to one often populated by drunks and those without work.

"I've a friend who owes me a favor. He sells various wares, traveling from one town to the next. I believe he's the perfect man to get you out of here in a discreet way."

Moving quickly to keep up, several questions lodged in her mind. She asked the most urgent one. "How much will he ask for the inconvenience of taking me along?"

Stopping at the back door of the boardinghouse, he looked at her. "Don't worry about that now, girl."

She touched his arm. "I need to know I have enough to pay him."

Ignoring her, Joe turned the knob, stepping into a long hallway. Walking past a couple doors, he knocked on the third one. "Carl. Are you in there?"

The sound of shuffling feet preceded the door opening. A rotund man with mussed hair and a thin, graying mustache stood there. "It's a bit early for a visit, isn't it, Joe?" The brusque question came with a slight sparkle in the man's eyes. "And who do you have with you?"

"It's close to noon, Carl. This is Lia. She needs to get out of town." Joe leaned toward his friend. "Right away."

Although his brows drew together, he stepped around Joe, making a slight bow. "It's a pleasure, Lia."

Gripping her hands together, she forced a tight smile. "Hello, Mr...."

"Carl is just fine." He looked back at Joe. "Where is it you'd like me to take her?"

"Where are you going next?"

Scratching his chin, Carl's mouth twisted. "Thought I'd go north. I haven't been to Settlers Valley in quite a spell." He shifted toward Lia. "We can leave this afternoon. We'll need to stop for the night. You'll sleep in the wagon...if that is agreeable."

Lia's breath caught at the name of the town close to Blaine's ranch. "That would be wonderful."

Joe didn't show any reaction to the hint of excitement in her voice. "Can she stay here until you leave?"

"Of course. My wagon is almost packed."

"I can help." Her eagerness brought a flicker of amusement to Joe's eyes.

"I'd appreciate any help you want to provide, Lia."

"And I'd be happy to pay you."

Carl held up a hand. "No need for that. As I recall, I owe Joe a favor." He looked at his friend. "If you're agreeable to me paying it off this way, we'll call it even."

Joe held out his hand. "Agreed." Shaking Carl's hand, he turned to Lia. "I'm going back to the Gold Dust. I want to find out if our *mutual friends* have taken rooms. Perhaps they're just passing through on their way back home." He stared at her a moment longer than needed, hoping she understood his meaning.

Stepping next to him, she touched Joe's arm. "Will you return before I leave?"

"I can't promise, but I will get word to you if our friends are only here for a meal with no plans to stay."

"Then I'd better thank you now, in case I don't see you before leaving." Rising to her toes, Lia placed a kiss on his cheek. "I don't know how I'll ever be able to repay you."

A slight blush crept up his face as a shy grin formed. "Send me a letter on how you're doing. Knowing you're safe and doing well is all the thanks I need." Slipping past her, Joe stopped at the door. "You take good care of her, Carl."

"I will."

Carl stood in the doorway of the enclosed peddler's wagon. Taking one more look around, he wiped his hands down his pants before glancing at Lia. "I believe that is all we'll need."

Standing at the bottom of the portable stairs he'd built to climb into and out of the wagon, she nodded, hearing someone coming up beside her.

"Are you going somewhere, Carl?"

Turning at the familiar voice, he nodded. "On my way north to Settlers Valley, Warren."

Lia shifted enough to see a man in his late twenties standing next to her. He smelled of smoke and liquor, his clothes stained and torn in several places.

"My name is Warren, ma'am. I don't believe we've met." His gaze wandered from the bonnet tied below her chin to the hem of her dress, an appreciative grin on his face. The action had her taking a step away.

"It's nice to meet you, Warren." Backing up, she put more distance between them.

"Is there something you want before I leave?" Carl rested a hand on the doorframe of the wagon.

Warren dragged his gaze away from her, looking up to focus his attention on Carl. "I'm in a little trouble. I, uh, wondered if you might be able to spare me a little money until you get back to town."

Carl looked at the steps, making no move to climb out of the wagon. "As I recall, you still owe me for the last time you borrowed money."

"I don't need much. A few dollars. I'll pay it back, plus what I borrowed last time, when you come back."

Shaking his head, Carl scowled. "Not this time, Warren. I'm short myself. That's why the trip to Settlers Valley."

"There's no one else who'll help me." Warren's anxious voice rose with each word.

Carl let out a breath, glaring down at him. "I told you there'd come a time when your gambling would get you into trouble. You should've stopped before it went this far."

Scrubbing a hand down his face, Warren's voice became desperate. "You don't understand. The man I owe will kill me if I don't pay him."

Carl's back stiffened. "Then maybe you should get out of town until you've had a chance to earn back what you owe. I'm sorry, Warren, but it's not my place to bail you out every time your gambling gets out of control." Glancing at the stairs, Carl let go of his hold on the doorframe, taking the first step to the ground.

Mumbling a series of oaths, Warren lashed out, kicking the portable steps as Carl balanced on the second step. A short cry sounded an instant before his arms flailed and his body twisted, foot catching before he toppled to the ground with a sickening thud.

"Carl!" Lia ran to him, kneeling to see his face contorted in pain.

"I think my ankle is broken," he ground out, trying to sit up and falling back onto the ground.

"Let me look at it. Can you straighten your legs for me?"

Gritting his teeth, Carl stretched out.

"Which ankle hurts?"

Carl pointed. "The right one."

"I need to remove your boot, Carl." Doing her best not to hurt him further, she pulled it off, checking for broken bones. After a few moments, she looked down at his face. "You didn't break anything, but your right ankle is swelling and beginning to turn color. I believe it's sprained."

"We should get him into his room."

Lia looked up to see Warren staring at them. "I think you've done enough."

Waving off her scathing remark, he bent down. "He can't walk, and you can't support him. I'll help Carl inside, then get one of the docs to look at him."

He was right. She couldn't bandage his ankle in the alley behind the boardinghouse. "Fine. Help him into his room so I can take care of bandaging the sprain."

"But—"

"I assure you, I can do what's needed," she interrupted. "Please, help him inside."

Warren didn't argue further before bending down next to Carl. "I'll need your help if we're going to do this." When Carl nodded, he helped him into a sitting position. "If I support your right side, do you think you can stand?"

"I suppose I'll have to." Grimacing, he rested his arm over Warren's shoulders, letting the younger man lift him up.

Supporting Carl's right side, Warren helped him to the boardinghouse and into his room. Settling him on the bed, he stepped away.

Lia pulled up Carl's pant leg, biting her lip before glancing toward Warren. "Can you get the bowl of water while I find something to bandage his ankle?"

Threading fingers through his hair, he nodded. "Sure." Warren walked to the nightstand, picking up the pitcher of water and bowl.

"Sorry, Lia."

Her brows drew together. "For what, Carl?"

"We'll not be able to leave as planned."

Shaking her head, she placed a hand on his shoulder. "Don't worry about that right now. Do you have anything I can use to bind your ankle?"

"There are rags in the closet. Will they be sufficient?"

A slight smile curved her lips. "They'll have to be."

An hour later, Lia sat on a chair next to the bed, watching Carl sleep. He'd consumed a good deal of whiskey while she wrapped his leg. She figured he might be out for the rest of the day.

Across the room, Warren stood at the window, hands shoved into the pockets of his pants.

"Were you planning to go with Carl to Settlers Valley?" He kept his back to her.

"Yes."

"Why not wait for the stage? It will come through here later in the week." Turning, he looked at her.

Not meeting his gaze, she leaned forward, fiddling with the edge of the coverlet on Carl's bed. "I need to leave right away."

He snorted, walking toward her. "It appears you won't be going anywhere very soon."

Loud pounding had Warren stepping to the door, pulling it open.

"Who are you, and where's Carl?"

Jumping up, Lia hurried to the door. "Joe, come in."

Brushing past Warren, his gaze landed on the bed. "What happened?"

"Carl sprained his ankle. I've bandaged it, but..." Lia shrugged. "Did you find out any more about our, um...friends?"

Joe let out a weary breath. "I'm afraid they'll be staying several days."

Shoulders slumping, she lowered herself into a chair. "And now I can't leave."

Warren crossed his arms, looking between the two. "If you need to get out of town, I can take you."

Joe's head snapped toward him. "Who in the hell are you?"

"A friend of Carl's."

"Joe, this is Warren. He and Carl were speaking just before the, well...the accident."

Looking him up and down, Joe's gaze narrowed on him. "How come I've never seen you before now?"

Warren didn't allow his irritation to show. "Couldn't tell you."

"I own the Gold Dust. Most people show up there at some point."

"I'm not much for spending money in a fancy restaurant."

Joe's eyes widened. "I don't run some fancy place."

"I wouldn't know." Warren's gaze locked on Lia. "If you want to get to Settlers Valley, I'll take you. If not, I'll be leaving now." Turning, he stopped at Lia's plea.

"Wait." Standing, she clasped her hands together. "Would you really take me to Settlers Valley?"

"I said I would." A dark expression crossed his face. "But you'll have to pay me."

Joe straightened. "How much?"

Rubbing his chin, Warren took a moment before quoting a price.

"That's ridiculous," Joe spat out.

Warren looked at Lia. "Do you own a horse?"

She shook her head.

"Food?"

Swallowing, she shook her head again.

"Bedroll, canteen, something to wear if it rains?"

Scowling, she threw up her hands, then pointed to the satchel in the corner. "Everything I own is in that bag."

"That's not going to get you to Settlers Valley."

Jaw tightening, Joe moved forward, reaching into a pocket. "Fine."

Lia stepped between the men. "You're not paying for my trip, Joe. Warren, I'll give you a third now for the horse and provisions, but not another cent until we reach Settlers Valley."

Snorting, he crossed his arm. "You expect me to trust you?"

"As much as I trust you."

Joe's hostile expression pinned Warren. "If Lia says she's got the money to pay you, she does."

"Fine. A third now, the rest the minute we get to Settlers Valley. Once we're there, you're on your own, lady."

She crossed her arms. "I keep the horse, saddle, tack, and bedroll."

His gaze hardened. "If you don't pay up when we get there..."

Joe moved to within inches of Warren's face. "She'll make good on her promise to pay you. When can you leave?"

Chapter Eight

Boar's Rock Ranch

Blaine smiled, looking up to read the new sign at the entrance to the ranch. "It's a good name, lads. Ewan and Ian will be pleased that it honors the MacLaren battle cry." Pulling out his six-shooter, he fired a shot into the air, shouting the cry in his native tongue. *"Creag an Tuirc!"*

Caleb sent a shot into the air. *"Creag an Tuirc!"*

Nate followed the other two in firing his gun. "To the Boar's Rock Ranch. May it have a long and successful future."

The ranch hands stood in two groups. The original men from Circle M in one, the Dempsey brothers in the other, all glancing at each other with a combination of confusion and amusement.

Blaine looked at those gathered around. "Heather and Geneen should have supper ready by now. Tonight, we'll celebrate naming the ranch. Be careful of imbibing in too much whiskey, lads. Tomorrow, we'll be up at dawn to finish the barn." He turned to Caleb and Nate. "Will you be staying here tonight or riding back to Highlander Ranch?"

"We'll need to ride back. Nate must be in town tomorrow, and I've a full day's work ahead of me. I'm grateful Heather's health is good as I need both her and

Geneen right now." Caleb scratched his chin, a grim expression crossing his face. "I do appreciate the two men Brodie sent out. It's just..."

Blaine clasped Caleb's shoulder. "We all know you want to do this on your own, lad, but Ewan and Ian made their wishes clear. They'll pay the wages until after the first cattle drive."

Caleb shook his head. "I don't know if I'll be able to afford them even after we deliver the cattle to market. It's an expense I hadn't planned."

Dropping his hand from Caleb's shoulder, Blaine glanced back up at the sign. "Don't be worrying yourself about it now. Tonight, we'll celebrate. You'll have time to consider what's best over the next few weeks."

Nate watched as the ranch hands rode toward the house. "As Heather's time gets closer, she won't be able to do as much as she can now, Caleb. I'll be able to help, but not as much as you'll need. You're going to need those two men more than you think."

Letting out an anxious breath, Caleb offered a bleak expression. "I suppose you're right."

"Remember, we still don't know if the fire was intentional or an accident. I'm glad for the extra men to help guard the women." Nate settled his hat lower on his forehead. "Anyone hungry?"

Walking to their horses, the three mounted, reining toward the house.

"Do you still think the fire was deliberate, Blaine?"

Moving at a slow pace, he nodded. "Aye, Nate. I'm certain of it."

"How can you be so sure?"

"I've something to show both of you."

Reining Galath to a pasture behind the original barn, he headed toward a patch of scorched brush. Stopping, he slid to the ground, stalking behind the burnt scrub. He stooped, grabbing what appeared to be a branch, lifting it up.

Joining him, Nate took the stick from his hand, studying the ball of blackened cloth at the top. "A torch."

"Aye." Blaine's nostrils flared. "I've found only the one. There could be more."

Nate held the branch up. "It wouldn't take more than this to set a fire. And it would've taken a single man, not a group."

Caleb rubbed the back of his neck. "Are you saying we could be looking for one man who has a grudge against Blaine?"

Nate nodded. "Or a woman."

Blaine's eyes widened for an instant before he threw his head back and laughed. "A lass?"

Although Nate's mouth lifted at the corners, his features remained stoic. "You don't believe a woman could set a barn on fire? I'm dead certain Heather, Geneen, or any number of MacLaren women are capable of burning a building down."

Calming down, Blaine choked out a final laugh. "Aye, they could...for the right reason."

Caleb crossed his arms, staring at the blackened torch. "Whether a man or woman did it, we need to find the reason. If we know why, we can figure out who."

Nate walked to his horse, tying the branch to the back of the saddle. "It could still be those cowboys we drove out of town a couple months ago. They were here for a specific reason."

"Aye, to intimidate the sellers not to make a deal with the MacLarens."

Caleb rubbed his brow. "Nate, you've been here the longest. Have you heard of other fires like this one?"

Eyes narrowing, his mouth twisted as he considered the question. "A new building not far from Mrs. Keach's boardinghouse burned down about a month before you and Heather were married. No one ever figured out how it started. Then there was the fire in a stable south of town. The farmer put it out real quick. That one started when his son kicked over a kerosene lantern." Rubbing his chin, Nate shook his head. "That's all I remember."

Grabbing Galath's reins, Blaine swung into the saddle, waiting for the others to mount. "Now that I know it was deliberate, my lads will be watching. You need to make sure the lads at your ranch do the same, Caleb."

Touching his heals to Nomad's side, he moved out alongside the others. "I'm going to speak with Marcus. He may have heard rumors."

"If we're talking rumors, you should also speak to Dahlia Keach." Caleb chuckled as he thought of the older woman who made it her duty to know everybody's business. "She's the queen of knowing what's going on in town."

Nate nodded. "Good idea. I'll also have a word with Benji at the Lucky Lady."

Their conversation stalled as they approached the house. Staying in the saddle as the others dismounted, Blaine looked around. The extra men would help, but he sure wished he had someone who could stay close to the house when he and the men worked the cattle. He didn't have the need or money for a housekeeper or cook.

Sliding to the ground, Blaine removed his hat, swiping an arm across his forehead. Somewhere in town was a person who needed work and would be more than happy to keep watch while the men tended the cattle. He'd speak to Nate about it.

"We'll bed down here for the night." Warren stopped alongside the Feather River. His demeanor had changed since they'd ridden out of Conviction. The somewhat congenial, almost charming façade deteriorated over each mile, becoming surly and threatening.

Lia had always traveled with a knife hidden in her reticule. Before leaving town, Joe had insisted she also carry a gun and a few rounds of ammunition. She'd balked at first, but was now grateful he'd insisted.

After listening to Warren's sometimes incoherent ramblings as they continued on the trail, Lia couldn't help wondering if he might attempt to steal the small amount of funds she'd hidden in her belongings. Patting the pocket of her dress, feeling the outline of the gun, she let out a breath, comforted to have it near.

It didn't take long for them to set out their bedrolls and eat the food he'd stashed in the saddlebags. Standing, she brushed the crumbs from her dress and headed toward the river.

"Where do you think you're going?" The harsh tone and scowl on Warren's face had her stopping.

Crossing her arms, Lia frowned. "Unless you have an objection, I need to wash up before retiring for the night."

"Don't be gone long."

Ignoring him, she continued the short distance to the edge of the river. Kneeling, she scooped up several handfuls of water, washing her face and hands before lifting her skirt to dry off.

The Feather River north of Conviction bore little resemblance to the churning waters along the docks when a large steamship stopped. These ships unloaded supplies and passengers, then turned around for the trip back to Sacramento. Only smaller steamers continued upriver. From what she'd heard, perhaps one ship a week traveled to Settlers Valley.

If she'd had the luxury of time, Lia would've considered waiting for the next ship north. The passage would've been less than the cost of the mare Joe helped Warren select, but the risk of being discovered would've been too great.

"Are you daydreaming again?"

Startling at the harsh voice, she jumped up and whirled around. "I'm paying you to take me to Settlers Valley, Warren. That doesn't include you following me."

Crossing his arms, Warren looked her up and down, smirking. "It includes whatever I say it does."

Disgusted at his tone and attitude, Lia brushed past him, stomping back up the trail. Removing her shoes, she slipped into her bedroll. The sooner she found sleep, the less time she'd have to deal with him before the final hours of their journey tomorrow.

Once in Settlers Valley, Lia would pay Warren and never have to see him again.

Eyes popping open, Lia blinked several times before remembering why she lay in a bedroll on the ground. Slipping back under the covers, she closed her eyes, sparing no thought as to why she wakened in the middle of the night. A moment later, her breath caught at the sound of men's voices.

"Warren?"

"Quiet." The hissed word was accompanied by soft rustling as he emerged from his bedroll.

Peeking out from under her cover, her eyes widened at the rifle in his hand. Without the slightest warning, he jumped up, firing a shot into the air.

"The next one will be through your chest," he yelled, crouching behind a thick tree trunk.

Untangling herself from the bedroll, Lia slid out, hurrying to stoop beside Warren. "Who is it?"

"How the hell do I know? Stay here." Leaving her behind, he raced toward the horses. Another shot rang out amid angry shouts before she heard the sound of retreating horses. "Damn thieves." Warren stomped back toward her. "They almost made off with the horses."

Standing, Lia hurried back to her bedroll, pushing aside a blanket in search for her reticule and satchel. Gasping, she clasped a hand to her chest.

"What is it?" Warren stepped next to her.

"My satchel and reticule. I can't find them."

Pulling out a cheroot, Warren lit it, shrugging. "They're here somewhere."

"They'd better be. All my money is in a pouch in the satchel."

Eyes going wide, Warren dropped the cheroot in the dirt, crushing it with the heel of his boot. Glancing around, he started searching the rest of the camp, looking behind trees and under bushes as Lia did the same. A few minutes later, he emerged from behind a thick, thorny shrub, holding the satchel in his hand.

"Oh, thank goodness." Running to him, she snatched it from his hand, setting the satchel on the ground and kneeling beside it. Opening the bag, she dug through the contents, then began frantically pulling items out. "Where is it?" Lia mumbled to herself.

"Where's what?"

Biting her lip, she didn't answer, continuing to search the bag.

His voice hardened. "Where is what?"

Her throat tightened, realizing an uncomfortable truth. If Warren knew her money had been stolen, he'd leave her stranded miles from their destination. She had no doubt he'd take the horse and saddle as payment, not sparing a moment of pity at her predicament.

"Here it is. All is fine." Grabbing the items she'd tossed aside, Lia stuffed them back into her bag. Standing, she let out a breath. "Did they take anything?"

He studied her, his gaze narrowing at the way she refused to look at him. Jaw tightening, Warren shook his head. "They were after the horses. I scared them off before they could set them loose." Looking to the east, he groaned. "It's almost sunup. Might as well pack up and get started. If we keep moving, we should be in Settlers Valley by early afternoon."

Pushing aside the fear at what would happen when they reached their destination, Lia prepared to leave. She didn't know what Warren would do when he discovered all her money had been taken. No matter how angry he got, she was certain he'd listen to reason, allowing her to get a job and pay him off. There truly wasn't much more he could do.

Shrugging off her concern, Lia mounted, reminding herself within a few hours she'd be facing a new and hopefully brighter future.

Boar's Rock Ranch

Pounding the last nail into place, Blaine set down the hammer. "That's it, lads." Testing the hinges on the door, he pulled it closed, then pushed it open, a tired smile forming on his face.

"It's a fine barn." Cal walked inside, taking a critical look around.

"Aye." Blaine wiped dirty hands down his pants. "The fire may have been a blessing. This one's bigger with larger stalls, a tack room, and tool storage."

"What now, boss?" Cal picked up the hammer and extra nails. Since he and his brothers had arrived, Cal had taken a leadership role, winning over the younger men who'd arrived from Circle M.

"Two of the lads will stay here to keep watch and load the rest of the tack in the barn. The rest of us will move the herd to another pasture. You and your brothers will go with me."

Cal picked up two halters, walking beside him as they headed to a nearby corral to get their horses. "I heard you mention you're interested in buying a bull."

"Aye. I'll be needing one soon. Caleb heard of one for sale at a ranch south of town. I plan to ride down there later today."

Cal glanced at him. "I used to buy bulls for the ranch we worked in New Mexico. You want me to ride along?"

Blaine thought a moment, pursing his lips before nodding. "Aye. I'd appreciate hearing what you think of him. We'll stop in town on the way back, have a drink with Nate."

"The sheriff?" Cal handed him one of the halters before opening the gate.

"Aye. He's been asking around about the fire. Maybe he'll have some news."

Blaine had told his men about finding the crudely made torch in the brush. They'd spent an hour speculating about who would want to destroy the barn and why they hadn't set fire to the house. They'd come up with nothing.

"The men will make certain it doesn't happen again, boss."

Slipping the harness on Galath, Blaine led him out of the corral and toward the barn. Cal walked beside him with his horse, neither speaking as they saddled their mounts.

Placing his left boot in the stirrup, Cal smoothly settled himself into the saddle. "Do you want me to ride out and send a couple of the men back to keep watch?"

Swinging into the saddle, Blaine nodded. "Two of the lads from Circle M. I'm going to make a quick circle around the house. When the lads arrive, I'll be joining you."

He waited until Cal rode north, disappearing down the trail before starting his trek around the property. Blaine shifted in the saddle, looking for anything out of place or suspicious. The entire situation mystified him. He hadn't been in town long enough to make enemies.

His gut told him the cowboys who'd been sent to outbid the MacLarens were long gone. None of the three had been seen in Settlers Valley since being run out of town by Nate. Besides, burning down a barn would do little to drive anyone out. Setting fire to the house wouldn't have done much, either.

Rustling or killing cattle would've had a bigger impact. Still, losing a few animals didn't bother Blaine as much as losing horses or a bull. He knew what the rancher wanted for his prized bovine and it was no small sum.

Blaine had already sent word to Ewan and Ian about the animal, getting their approval to buy him if he could come to terms with the rancher. He had no doubt they'd reach an agreement. The issue wasn't settling on a reasonable price.

What worried Blaine was keeping the bull safe once they got the animal to Boar's Rock Ranch.

Chapter Nine

Settlers Valley

Lia groaned with relief, her back and bottom hurting from hours in the saddle. It had taken longer than expected with Warren's horse catching a rock in his hoof several miles from town. They'd finished the last of their hardtack and cold beans, letting the horse rest before finishing the journey. Within an hour, the sun would set and darkness would veil the town.

Her tired body didn't stop her from inspecting the buildings as they rode down the main street. From what she could see, it was the only street in the small town.

She'd refused to let herself dwell on what would happen once Warren learned about her lack of funds. Lia decided she'd calmly explain what happened and suggest she get a job to pay him back. If that didn't work, she'd sell the horse and tack, which would leave her enough to live on until she found a job. After all, what else could he do?

"Perhaps we'll find rooms there." Lia pointed to a sign. Settlers Valley Boardinghouse. "We could clean up and get supper." Reining her horse to a stop, she slid off the saddle.

"Hold up. First I get paid, then we find rooms and eat."

Heart sinking, her hand tightened on the reins. Forcing herself to remain calm, she pushed aside the cold ball of dread in her stomach. Opening her mouth, she clamped it shut at the sound of a door opening.

"You two looking for a room?"

Lia tore her gaze from Warren to look at an older woman standing in the doorway of the boardinghouse. She spoke before he had a chance. "Two rooms, if you have them."

"I only have one."

Warren cleared his throat. "We'll figure this out later. Right now, I want what you owe me."

Lia cast a furtive glance at the woman, her chest squeezing. "Thank you, Mrs..."

"Dahlia Keach. I own this establishment." She looked between the two, instincts warning her of trouble. "Why don't you come inside and I'll get your name so you don't lose the room."

Relief flooded her. "That would be wonderful." Lia ignored Warren's mumbled curse as she followed Dahlia inside.

"What's your name, dear?"

"Permilia Jacobs, ma'am."

"That your husband?" Dahlia glanced over Lia's shoulder.

Lia shuddered at the thought. "No, ma'am. I, um...paid him to bring me here." Hearing the door open, she didn't turn around, praying it wasn't Warren.

"You gotta settle with me before you go paying for a room."

She cringed at the unforgiving tone, seeing Dahlia's eyes flash as he stepped beside her. Lia lifted the satchel onto the counter. Opening it, she sifted through the bag, already knowing there'd be no pouch filled with money. Feeling a flash of nausea, she closed the bag, turning to face him.

"I have a confession."

Jaw tightening, his face flushed. "You'd better not tell me you agreed to this without having the money."

She lifted her chin. "I had the money...every penny. The men who came to our camp last night must've stolen it."

Placing fisted hands on his hips, Warren let loose with a string of curses.

Dahlia crossed her arms, her voice stern. "We'll have none of that in my house, young man."

"I don't care what you do or don't allow. This lady owes me for bringing her from Conviction and I mean to get paid."

Dahlia glared at him. "I don't know how you expect her to pay if she has no money."

"Truly, Warren. I had the money when we left. That's why you found the satchel in the bushes. Those men robbed me before trying to steal the horses."

Glowering at Lia, Warren gripped her arm. "I don't care how you lost it. You owe me, and you're going to pay." He looked at Dahlia. "Where's that room?"

"No!" Lia tried to yank her arm away, wincing when his hold tightened.

Slapping her hands on the counter, Dahlia leaned toward him. "There'll be none of that in this establishment."

Jerking Lia to him, he lowered his face to within an inch of hers. "You owe me, and you're damn well going to pay."

Panic ripped through her at his unyielding gaze. "Can't we talk about this, Warren?"

"We've talked enough." Tugging her to the door, he sent a warning glare at Dahlia. "And you're not to interfere."

Her jaw dropping, Dahlia moved to walk around the counter when Warren pulled his gun.

"I'm warning you. Stay out of this."

Slamming the door behind them, his fingers dug into her skin as he looked up and down the street. A feral grin tilted the corners of his mouth. "The Lucky Lady. That's how you'll pay me." He dragged her beside him, crossing the street.

"What...what do you mean?"

He didn't look at her, pulling her onto the boardwalk. "You belong to me, Miss Permilia Jacobs. And before the night's over, you're going to understand what that means."

Running outside, Dahlia wrung her hands. Her heart twisted as she watched Warren drag Lia toward the Lucky Lady. Dashing across the street, she waited until they'd gone through the doors of the saloon before running toward the jail, throwing the door open.

"Sheriff, you have to come quick."

Nate looked up from reading the stack of wanted posters on his desk. "What is it this time, Mrs. Keach?"

"A horrible man dragged a nice young woman into the Lucky Lady. I don't know what he plans, but I can tell you it's evil."

Nate worked to keep the grin off his face. "Evil?"

"I mean it, Sheriff. The man is quite wicked and is forcing his attentions on the girl." She glanced out the window. "There's no telling what he plans for her."

"How do you know they're not married and having some kind of quarrel?"

"Believe me, that is not the case. He agreed to bring her to Settlers Valley—for money." She lifted a brow on the last.

Nate rubbed a brow, sighing. "And?"

"They were robbed on the way here. All her money was taken, but that man is insisting she still pay. Who knows what he has planned, but I'm telling you, it's not good. You need to get over there before it's too late."

Shaking his head, Nate pushed up from his chair. "All right. Let's go see what wicked ideas this man has." He looked down at the gun nestled in the holster, glad he hadn't taken the belt off. With only one hand, it was a little bit of a chore to get it around his waist and buckled. Opening the door, he motioned for her to go ahead of him.

"I'm coming with you."

He shook his head. "I don't think that's such a good idea."

Crossing her arms, she glared at him. "It's not as if I've never been in a saloon, Sheriff."

"I didn't mean to imply you haven't, Mrs. Keach."

Dropping her arms, she turned toward the saloon. "Then it's settled. I'll accompany you inside."

Stifling a groan, Nate led the way, stopping outside the saloon. "Are you certain you want to go inside?"

Jutting her chin out, Dahlia nodded. "Absolutely."

"All right." Pushing the door open, he waited until she entered, then stepped in beside her. "Where are they?"

She nodded toward a table in the corner. Three men played cards. Behind one of them stood a young woman, her expression drawn in misery. "Right there. She's standing behind the man who forced her into the saloon."

"Why don't you wait for me here?" Nate guessed the answer before the question was out of his mouth.

"I wouldn't consider it."

Blowing out a breath, he took a step forward. "Do not say anything until I've had a chance to figure out what's going on." When she cleared her throat to argue, he pinned her with a hard glare. "I mean it, Mrs. Keach. You'll stand by the bar and let me do my job."

Mouth twisting in disappointment, she gave a curt nod. "Fine. But I'll be watching."

"I'm sure you will," Nate mumbled.

"What was that?"

"Nothing, Mrs. Keach. Now, go find a place at the end of the bar and wait."

Moving toward the table, he nodded at a couple men he knew. Standing behind an open chair, his features softened when his gaze lit on the young woman.

She was lovely, with shiny brown hair and the most unique eyes he'd ever seen. Turquoise with splashes of brown with golden specks. If he wasn't happily married to Geneen, he might've considered learning more about her. Instead, his gaze moved to the man in front of her, who looked up at him.

"You want to join us, Sheriff?"

"Not right now. I don't recall seeing you in town before. I'm Sheriff Hollis."

Not taking his eyes off the cards in his hand, he nodded. "Warren."

"Do you have a last name, Warren?"

"Not one I'm proud of sharing." He tossed a couple cards onto the table. "Two." Picking up his whiskey, he took a sip.

"Is there a reason you've got a young woman standing behind you?"

Warren lifted a brow. "She's my business, not yours."

"I'm making her my business."

Tossing down his cards, Warren leaned back. "She belongs to me."

"Perhaps you haven't heard. The war is over, along with the ability to own someone else."

Before Warren could respond, the doors burst open. Two men walked inside, laughing. Searching the room, one of them raised a hand in greeting when he spotted Nate.

"We just came from the jail, lad." Blaine clasped him on the shoulder. "You remember Cal."

Nate nodded at both. "I've got a little situation I need to deal with, then I'll join you at a table."

Blaine's eyes narrowed on Nate before his gaze moved to the table in front of them. Traveling from one man to another, he stopped on one he didn't recognize. The man's eyes were locked on him.

"I was just telling the sheriff why the little chit belongs to me."

Blaine's head lifted, his mouth going slack, eyes wide when he recognized the trembling woman. "Lia?" His throat thickened at the sight of a single tear falling down her cheek.

Warren barked out a humorless laugh. "Ah, I see you know her. Then you probably also know she's a liar and a cheat."

Anger building, Blaine lunged at the man, stopping when Nate and Cal grabbed his arms. Nate moved to stand in front of him, shifting his attention to Warren.

"I believe you were about to tell me why you brought her into the saloon."

Warren laid down his cards, grinning as he scooped his winnings into a pile. "For this." He indicated the growing mound. "As soon as I have enough to pay for a room, I'm taking her back to the boardinghouse."

Blaine's face, mottled with rage, raised to hers. "You agreed to this?"

Lia shook her head, her features heavy with humiliation. "No...yes. I've no way to pay my debt." Lowering her face into her hands, a sob burst from her throat.

"She agreed all right, the same as any good Mormon girl would." Warren glanced over his shoulder at her. "Your duty is to obey the commands of those over you, right, sweetheart?"

Nostrils flaring, Blaine pulled out a chair, leaning toward Warren. "How much does she owe?"

Warren named a figure. When Blaine reached into a pocket, he laughed. "I'll not let you pay her debt. She's the one who will pay me back. In full."

Blaine ignored Lia's gasp. "Then I'll make you a wager."

Warren's brows drew together. "A wager?"

"Aye. We draw one time. You get the high card, I leave."

Warren's eyes flared with interest. "And if you get the high card?"

"I leave with the lass...and her debt is paid in full."

Throwing his head back, Warren laughed. "That's it? If I win, you walk out."

"Aye."

"You must think me a complete fool."

Blaine didn't respond, waiting for what he believed would be a counteroffer.

Warren picked up the deck of cards, shuffling them. "If I win, I keep the girl, plus you pay me a hundred dollars." Continuing to shuffle, one corner of his mouth tilted into a malicious grin. "If you get the high card, you leave with the girl."

A moment passed, Blaine seeming to consider the offer. "Anything else?"

"No."

Blaine looked at Nate and Cal, then turned back to Warren. "Agreed."

"Excellent." Shuffling the deck one more time, Warren set it on the table.

Face impassive, Blaine's eyes locked on Warren's. "You first, lad."

He tossed back the last of his whiskey and chuckled. "Lad, is it? Fine." Reaching out, he cut the cards partway down, holding up the stack. "Queen of diamonds."

One of Lia's hands covered her mouth, the other settling on her stomach, doing all she could to ignore the growing nausea. Squeezing her eyes shut, she sent

110

up a prayer, a bleak sense of despair claiming her. Lia didn't know much about cards, but she did understand drawing a queen was as good as winning.

"Looks as if you'll be leaving here empty-handed...*lad*." Warren sneered the last word, looking behind him to wink at Lia.

The emotionless expression on Blaine's face didn't change as he reached out. Taking his cut, he took a quick look before holding it out for everyone to see.

The air left Warren's lungs. "King of hearts." Sucking in a breath, he slammed a hand on the table, then pointed at Blaine. "You cheated."

Setting the cards down, Blaine stood. "Your deck and you shuffled. I win, laddie."

Red with anger, Warren pushed himself up. Before he could grab Blaine, Nate moved beside him, twisting his arm behind his back. "Enough. He won a fair bet. Now you're going to sit down and let him leave with the woman. Her debt is paid in full."

Taking a moment to calm at least a portion of the anger still rolling through him, Blaine approached Lia, holding out his hand. "Come with me, lass." Before she could grasp it, Warren shifted toward them.

"She was a good little piece," he sneered. The next instant, Blaine's fist landed on his jaw. A small sense of satisfaction claimed him when Warren crumbled to the floor. It wasn't quite enough to dispel his rage at the entire situation.

Nostrils flaring, he grabbed Lia's hand, pulling her behind him.

"Blaine, I didn't—"

"Be quiet."

"But—"

Stopping, he whipped around, raising a finger. "Not another word, lass."

A ball of fear lodged in her chest. She'd never seen this side of him—the hard features, unbridled anger.

"Am I clear?"

Nodding, she blinked back tears, looking away.

"Good." He continued toward the door. "Do you have a horse?"

Her answer was a blank stare.

"It's in front of my boardinghouse." Blaine turned to see Dahlia at his side. "Poor thing." She touched Lia's shoulder. "He's an evil man. It was good of you to get her out of there."

"Her horse, Mrs. Keach?"

"Oh, yes. It's right over there. I'll go inside and retrieve her satchel."

Stopping next to the mare, he looked at Lia. "Is the mare yours?"

A bleak expression met his. "Yes."

Lifting her, he settled Lia in the saddle, then took the reins. Grabbing the satchel from Mrs. Keach, he murmured his thanks, continuing down the street to where Galath waited. In one smooth motion, he swung into the saddle, holding his horse's and the mare's reins.

"Where are we going?"

"To Boar's Rock." Pinching the bridge of his nose, a scowl covered Blaine's face, his voice hard and edgy. "Unless you've an emergency, I'll not be hearing another word from you."

Chapter Ten

Boar's Rock

Moonlight illuminated the sign as they rode past, catching Lia's attention. She thought it a strange name for a ranch, but refused to voice her question, fearing Blaine's reaction.

He hadn't spoken a word to her the entire trip, a journey taking much longer than she anticipated. He'd talked with Cal, even laughing a few times. The sound caused a lump to form in her throat, choking her with shame. If she had anywhere else to go, Lia would yank the reins from Blaine's hand and ride off as fast and far as possible.

Slumping in the saddle, she turned her gaze from the sign to what appeared to be a newly completed barn and a large house silhouetted in the moonlight. As they got closer, she saw what she guessed to be a bunkhouse. Several men stood outside, talking, rolling cigarettes, or smoking. All were bundled up in heavy coats. Looking at her tattered one, Lia wished she had the money for something warmer.

"You can get down now." She glanced down to see Blaine standing next to her. Ignoring the hands he held out to help her, she dismounted, moving several feet away from him.

"It won't be so easy getting away from me, lass. This is my place. The closest ranch is miles away." His controlled voice belied the waves of anger she felt rolling off him. She'd hoped the ride would've calmed him some. Apparently not.

"Highlander Ranch," she muttered.

His eyes widened. "So you were paying attention. Aye, it belongs to Caleb Stewart. He married my cousin, Heather. Nate and his wife, Geneen, live with them." Leaving her behind, he started walking toward the barn.

"I heard about them from your family."

Stopping, he whirled around. "What do you know of my family?"

Refusing to cower any longer, she straightened her back, eyes boring into his. "There was a, um...situation in town. Cam heard about it and took me to Circle M for a few days. I stayed in your mother's house."

"Did you now? And were you staying in Cam's room while you were there?" He grimaced at his harsh tone.

She gasped at the thoughtless accusation. "Of course not. Your mother had me stay in your room." Lia noticed his mouth quirk up at the corners before masking his features. Walking to her horse, she untied the satchel from the back of her saddle. "Will I be staying in the bunkhouse or barn?"

"You'll be in the house, with me."

"If you don't mind, I'd prefer the barn."

Dropping the reins, he stalked toward her, stopping less than a foot away. "I *do* mind, lass. Same as my family at Circle M, I saved you from another difficult situation, so you'll be doing as I say." A roguish grin tipped the corners of his mouth. "My room is at the top of the stairs. You're welcome to stay in there with me, lass."

Blaine had no idea how much she wanted to. If she had her way, he'd never learn the extent of her feelings for him. Lifting her chin, she pushed past him.

"I'll pick another room, Mr. MacLaren. Not to be brazen, but I don't believe you'd have any idea of what to do with me if I stayed in your room."

His jaw dropped open, the air whooshing from his lungs. Stalking behind her, he grabbed Lia's arm.

"What did you say?"

Refusing to look at him, she wrenched her arm out of his grasp. "I believe you understood me."

Catching her chin with his fingers, he forced her to meet his hard stare. "I do believe you've underestimated me. When I've calmed down from all the shenanigans you've pulled, we'll be talking about just how much you've misjudged me...and my intentions."

Sucking in a breath, Lia slapped his arm away, refusing to allow Blaine to intimidate her.

"I'll say my goodnights now, Mr. MacLaren." She took a few steps before turning back to face him, offering an angelic smile. "Sweet dreams."

Blaine paced back and forth in what would soon be his study, a glass of whiskey in his hand—the third one, if he were counting.

Riding into town with Cal after a successful negotiation for a bull he expected would be the foundation of the ranch's breeding program, his spirits were higher than they'd been in weeks. Not finding Nate at the jail, their next stop had been the Lucky Lady. A couple drinks and a few hands of cards would be the perfect way to unwind before riding back to Boar's Rock.

His mood crashed the instant he spotted Lia in the saloon, hands clasped together, her woeful expression tearing at his heart. Whatever she'd done, it hadn't happened out of malice. She didn't have a smidgeon of dishonesty in her blood.

Swallowing the last of the whiskey in his glass, he poured another, uncaring about how he'd feel in the morning. Slumping into a threadbare chair, he rested his head against the back, the glass hanging between his fingers.

The woman he'd been unable to purge from his thoughts since meeting her in Conviction slept upstairs. Lia played on his mind from the time he awoke in the morning until falling into bed at night. Even then, her image plagued him, preventing sleep.

Blaine had planned to visit Lia when they drove the cattle to Circle M, hoping to convince her to move to Settlers Valley. More precisely, to Boar's Rock. He needed someone to prepare meals for the men, keep the house clean, and help with other chores.

Considering his idea now, Blaine realized the inappropriateness of such an arrangement. Even if his intentions were honorable, the odds of living up to them were small. It had taken seconds for his body to respond to her presence in the saloon. His reaction had been the same each time she was near him back home. Whether serving meals at the Gold Dust or passing him on the boardwalk, Blaine's reaction remained consistent. A fact he hated and treasured at the same time.

Swallowing the last of the whiskey, he set the glass down, closing his eyes. Blaine refused to climb the stairs to enter a bedroom a door away from where she slept. Staying downstairs seemed the safest option for them both.

Resting his legs on the ottoman, he allowed a ragged breath to escape. The days ahead would be long and tiring. The nights would be worse with Lia in the house. Regardless, he meant to keep her here.

First, he had to get the truth about her reasons for traveling to Settlers Valley. He hoped she'd come because of him, but his instincts told him there was much more behind the trip.

Recalling Warren mentioning her Mormon background, Blaine decided he'd start there. Lia had never spoken about her family. Then again, he'd never asked, satisfied to spend whatever time he could around her. He vowed tomorrow would be the day he rectified that oversight.

As the whiskey worked its way through his body, he allowed himself one more image of Lia before falling asleep. The same image he'd welcomed each night since moving away from Conviction. The difference was he now had the real thing a heartbeat away.

"It's none of your business." Lia flitted around the kitchen, searching for the staples she needed to prepare breakfast.

Placing fisted hands on his hips, the anger from yesterday returned to Blaine's face. "What do you mean it's none of my business?"

"Are you deaf or simply slow? My reasons for coming to Settlers Valley are mine alone." Picking up a spatula, she held it in the air. "Where are the eggs?"

Keeping out of reach of the makeshift weapon, Blaine backed up. "In the henhouse. You've actually got to fetch the eggs before you can cook them."

Setting down the spatula, she crossed her arms, her mouth twisted into a grim line. "Is that your way of being funny?"

He shrugged. "Is it working on you, lass?"

"No, it's not," she hissed. "You asked me to prepare breakfast for the men. How am I supposed to do that without the supplies and with your constant questions about my reasons for leaving Conviction?"

"Fine. I'll hold the questions until after breakfast." He pointed to a cupboard. "There's flour in the cupboard for biscuits, bacon and butter in the larder. Start with those. I'll get the eggs."

Blaine didn't wait for a response before walking out the back door. Lia watched from the window, her breath catching at the fine sight he made in his tight pants and shirt stretched over taut muscles earned from long hours of labor. Turning away, she chastised herself for taking any time to appreciate the man. He'd been nothing but a thorn in her side since finding her in the Lucky Lady. Now the arrogant rancher thought she owed him an explanation.

Pressing a finger against her temple to relieve the throbbing, she admitted Blaine did deserve an explanation about her sudden arrival in Settlers Valley—and for the way he found her. He'd witnessed Lia's complete humiliation, yet still rescued her from a fate she couldn't begin to describe.

Instead of thanking Blaine, she'd fought him. It had become her way of regaining a scant amount of pride after the shameful way he'd found her.

Stepping into the kitchen, Blaine set the basket of eggs on the counter. "Here you are, lass." A puzzled expression crossed his face as he scanned the room. "Were my directions on where to find everything too difficult?"

Renewed mortification flushed her face. Clenching both hands at her sides, Lia inhaled a deep breath.

"No, your directions were quite clear." Stepping to the cupboard, she pulled down the flour canister and mixing bowl. The larder proved a little more challenging. The knob refused to turn, even when she gripped it with both hands and pulled with all her strength. Straightening, ready to try again, she stilled at the feel of Blaine's hands resting on her waist.

"Let me get that for you, lass." His warm breath brushed against the sensitive skin below her ear. Feeling her tremble, he leaned down once more, skimming his lips against the soft column of her neck. "Lass?"

She'd never felt anything as wonderful as his powerful body pressed against hers, his breath hot against her skin. Breathing in ragged gasps, she leaned back, feeling the hard contours of his chest. Closing her eyes, she became aware of his hands moving to span her stomach.

Turning Lia to face him, he cupped her face with both hands. When she didn't move to pull away, Blaine bent down, brushing his lips against hers. Desire raced through him with the one brief touch, understanding the innocence she represented. Gazing at her trembling lips, her closed eyes, his passion spiked.

Skimming his lips across hers once more, he claimed her mouth, deepening the kiss when she wrapped her arms around his neck. For a woman without experience, he was stunned at the eagerness of her response. So lost in the way her soft curves molded to his lean body, he didn't hear anyone approach until someone coughed behind him.

Hearing her gasp, he broke the kiss, shielding Lia with his body when he turned to see who'd entered the room.

Cal kept his gaze locked on Blaine. "Sorry, boss, but the men are asking about breakfast."

Stepping from behind him, Lia touched a hand to her hair, clearing her throat. "Please let them know I'll have it ready in no time. And, um...tell them I'm sorry for the delay."

Touching a finger to his brow in a mock salute, Cal nodded. "Thank you, ma'am."

Blaine didn't move until he heard the front door close. Turning, he grasped Lia's arm before she could move away.

"That shouldn't have happened, lass." The confusion on her face stalled the rest of what he'd been about to say. "I mean, you're living in my house, helping with chores. It isn't suitable for me to take advantage of you as I did."

Blinking, she shook her head before a mischievous grin tipped the corners of her mouth. "Would it be more suitable if I took advantage of you?"

Her quick response caused Blaine's jaw to drop before he tipped his head back and laughed. "Ah, lass. I can already see how you're going to be quite the temptation."

Her face sobered. "One you intend to resist."

He studied her, wondering again at the reason for her traveling to Settlers Valley. "We've no time now, but when I return, we'll be sitting down and you'll be telling me the truth of why you're here."

Sucking in a breath, she took a step back. "But—"

He touched a finger to her lips. "And I'll have the truth, Lia. There'll never be any lies between us. Never."

She'd been glad when he'd left, allowing her to prepare breakfast in peace. Going through the familiar routine, she had biscuits baking within minutes. The sound of frying bacon helped calm her after what had been the most intense experience she'd ever had with a man.

Remembering how his lips caressed hers, she shuddered, touching shaky fingers to her mouth. Her first kiss, and it had been with the only man she'd ever desired.

Without a doubt, she knew her father and brother believed she'd been soiled long ago. Until that morning, she'd protected herself, never allowing anyone to get close or take advantage.

She'd been terrified when Warren threatened her, insisting he'd take payment in one of two ways—cash or her services. When she'd protested, saying she'd never been with a man, he laughed. Apparently her innocence meant little to him. She shuddered at what might have happened if Blaine hadn't appeared when he did, saving her from Warren's mortifying intentions.

Pushing the bacon around in the iron skillet, her lips twitched, realizing she'd welcome the same intentions by Blaine. Since the first time she'd been close to him, Lia knew he'd become a special person in her life.

Chuckling, she recalled the night he'd fallen down drunk on the boardwalk outside Buckie's Castle. She'd helped him to her room in the back of the Gold Dust, letting him sleep it off until his family arrived the following morning.

From then until he'd left for Settlers Valley, they'd been friends. His departure left her with an emptiness, a gap she couldn't close. Even with Warren's threat looming over her, seeing Blaine enter the saloon yesterday filled the vacant spot in her heart.

She didn't know how long he'd allow her to stay at the ranch—a few days, a week, a month. Whatever the time, Lia vowed to work for her keep each day until he sent her away.

"Are you ready, lass?"

Her throat tightened, face heating at the sound of the familiar voice. Scooping the eggs onto a plate, she picked it and the platter of bacon up, shifting to look at him. Nodding at the bowl filled with biscuits, she flashed him a shy grin.

"This will have to do for today. Tomorrow will be better." Meaning to move past him, she stopped when his hand gripped her arm.

"You've worked magic, lass. Whatever comes tomorrow will be the same." He stared at her a moment longer than necessary, knowing his words could mean many things.

The men sat around the dining and living rooms, tin plates in their hands, giving her appreciative smiles when she emerged from the kitchen.

"This is all there is." Setting the food on the table, she gestured toward the platters. "Get what you want before it gets cold." Pulling up a chair, she watched, fascinated by how fast they got to the table.

Within minutes, the food disappeared. She refused to take a plate for herself, content to watch them consume every morsel.

"What of you, lass?" Blaine sat down next to her. "Where's yours?"

"I'll get something when you leave."

Taking a bite, he chewed, his mind drifting to the work for today. "Cal and I will be retrieving the new bull today. I'll stop at the general store when we pass by town and pick up more supplies. Will, Newt, and the rest of the men will be in the northern pasture with the cattle. Will you be all right here alone while we're gone?" His face showed creases of worry she hadn't expected.

"I'll be fine. There's much I can do and the quiet will be nice." She said the last without thought. "I mean, it is a little rowdy with so many men around."

Chuckling, he ate the last of his food. "There's a rifle and ammunition by the front door. You do know how to shoot, don't you?"

"Of course."

Standing, he nodded at the rest of the men. "Good. Then we'll be off."

Telling them to leave their plates on the table, she followed them to the front door, watching as they mounted and rode out in separate directions. For the first time in weeks, a sense of calm settled over her. She didn't know what her future would bring, but right now, on this particular morning, life couldn't be better.

Chapter Eleven

"You made a good purchase, MacLaren." The elderly rancher extended his hand, clasping Blaine's. "I'd hoped not to sell him, but it wasn't to be." The man seemed to be lost in thought for a moment before glancing at Blaine again. "He belonged to my son. Raised him since birth. Young fool rode east to join Lincoln's Union Army not long after the war started." Shaking his head, he cleared his throat. "I never saw him again."

Cal walked up to the older man. "We lost many good men in the war. I'm sorry you had to experience it."

"Did you fight?"

His features blank, Cal nodded. "I did. For the Union Army, the same as your son."

Letting out a shaky breath, the rancher patted Cal's arm. "I'm glad you made it home." He switched his attention to Blaine. "As I said, take care of the bull. He'll serve you well."

"I assure you, he'll be well cared for. If you ever want to see him, you're welcome at Boar's Rock anytime." Blaine walked to his horse. Grabbing the reins, he looked at Cal. "We'd best be going. We've a long way before evening."

Raising a hand to the rancher in farewell, Blaine rode on one side of the over two thousand pound animal while Cal rode on the other. Herding the bull along the trail, each settled into their saddles, knowing they had miles to go at a slow pace.

An hour passed with little conversation. The bull continued his plodding pace, rarely lifting his head. Blaine's mind rested on Lia and what had happened before breakfast. He hadn't intended to kiss her, to pull her against his chest. The memory caused his body to harden, his blood to heat. If Cal hadn't walked in—

"Seems you knew the lass before seeing her at the saloon."

Cal's voice interrupted Blaine's self-indulgent thoughts.

"Aye. We met in Conviction. The lass, uh...saved me from making an eejit of myself. We became friends."

"That so?"

Blaine's eyes narrowed on him. "Aye, it's so."

"Did you invite her to join you here?"

Chuckling, Blaine shook his head. "Nae."

Cal waited a spell before speaking again. "Did you know she was coming?"

"Nae, I didn't."

"Then what do you plan to do with her?"

Massaging the back of his neck, Blaine let out a weary breath. "I don't know."

Beating the last of the large rugs, Lia released it from the clothesline, wrestling it into the house.

Dragging it through the kitchen, she felt the moisture build on her forehead. Pausing to swipe strands of hair from her face, she took a deep breath and pulled again.

She'd been cleaning for hours, ever since Blaine and his men left, washing up after breakfast before dusting the entire house, sweeping the floors, and now thrashing the rugs. The final one was the largest. She didn't know how much it weighed, but it was by far the heaviest of the bunch.

Stopping for a few seconds, Lia puffed out a tired breath, then gripped the rug again. Tugging it through the dining room, she dropped her hold in front of the sofa, her chest heaving. Glaring down at it, she crossed her arms.

"Thought you'd win, didn't you? Even an old rug isn't heavy enough to make me give up." Smiling to herself, Lia bent down, gripping a corner to pull it to the desired location. Laying it out, she stepped back, admiring her work.

Shifting a couple tables around, Lia pursed her lips, tilting her head to the side. Satisfied, she wiped her hands down an apron already dirty from a full day's work. Lifting her head, she sniffed the air.

The venison stew.

Hurrying to the kitchen, Lia grabbed a spoon, plunging it into the large pot and stirring. Her mouth twisting with indecision, she set the spoon down to pick up a ladle. Dipping it into a bucket by the stove, she scooped a full amount of water, pouring it into the pot.

Stirring the stew again, she tasted the mixture, nodding in satisfaction. Setting down the spoon, Lia grasped the only piece of jewelry she owned. The gold pocket watch with ivory face had belonged to her grandfather on her mother's side. He and Lia had been close, too close according to her father. Before the old man passed away, he'd secretly given Lia the watch, telling her in his own firm way not to let her father know.

As Lia grew older, she understood his meaning. Had her father ever learned she'd been given the watch, he would've taken it, accusing her of theft. A brisk shudder rushed through her at the thought, as happened most every time she thought of her father.

Checking the time, she slid it back into her pocket. "Time to prepare the biscuits," she muttered, opening the cupboard to retrieve the flour and mixing bowl.

Blending the ingredients, Lia glanced at the pies cooling on the rack, allowing her mind to wander once more. This time to Blaine and the kisses they shared. Throughout the day, she'd found herself wondering if he'd do it again. She wanted him to, hoped he would, but got the impression he regretted his actions. The notion caused her good mood to plummet.

Refusing to give in to the depressing thought, Lia opened the flour canister, spreading a good portion on the counter. Turning the biscuit mixture on top, she kneaded the dough with more enthusiasm than required before grabbing the rolling pin.

Before she could start rolling the dough, loud pounding on the front door had her setting the pin aside. Wiping her hands down the apron, Lia briefly wondered who might be calling this far from town. Blaine didn't mention neighbors, except...

Excitement coursed through her at the thought the relatives he mentioned, Heather and Geneen, might've come for a visit. Without looking through the window or picking up the rifle, she flung the door open.

Enthusiasm turned to fear at the sight of a man dressed in leather pants and shirt, wearing a hat in an intricate basket weave with tiny beads for decoration. Breath hitching, her hand came up to her throat, voice faltering when two more men came into view.

Indians.

Body tensing, she backed up, reaching for the rifle when her heel caught on a newly cleaned rug. An involuntary squeal pierced the air, her arms thrashing for purchase before she fell backward, hitting her head on the floor.

Blaine sucked on a piece of lemon candy he'd purchased at the general store, thinking of the small sack in the saddlebag containing the additional ones for Lia. They'd stopped in town long enough to grab a few supplies, garnering the stares of several passersby who gawked at the impressive bull. Standing at the counter, he'd spotted the jar of candy, remembering Lia talking about the candies her mother used to buy with the meager coin her father supplied.

Looking up at the clear sky, he estimated two more hours at their slow pace to reach the ranch. He'd hoped to stop by Highlander Ranch, show off the bull to Caleb, but time had slipped away. At their current speed, Lia would already have supper prepared when they arrived at Boar's Rock.

Keeping his attention on the animal and trail ahead, Blaine allowed himself to relax. Pondering how the bull could impact the fortunes of the ranch, he was unprepared for the gunfire hitting the dirt in front of him.

Startled, Blaine spotted blood on the bull's side at the same instant the animal panicked, charging ahead. Shouting at Cal to keep with the fleeing animal, Blaine drew his gun as another shot whizzed by, hitting him in the left shoulder.

Ignoring the pain, he shifted in the saddle, aiming at the outcropping of rocks behind them. Firing twice, he slid to the ground, slapping Galath on the rear as he searched the area for any sign of where the shooter hid. A flash of light drew his attention.

Sliding beneath a nearby bush, Blaine raised his gun, firing in the direction of the light. This time, he thought he heard a loud groan, followed by muttered curses. Staying hunkered down, he waited several minutes before pushing up, whistling for his horse.

Surveying the area, believing the shooter had been wounded and left, he swung into the saddle. Huddled down, Blaine nudged Galath into a gallop, determined to catch Cal and the bull. A hundred yards up the trail, he spotted them, the animal grazing while Cal stood watch, his rifle at the ready.

Drawing closer, Blaine examined the dried blood matting the bull's coat, relieved the bullet had only grazed him.

"Are you all right?" he called to Cal, who kept his gaze fixed on the trail behind them.

"It appears I'm doing better than you." Cal walked toward him, looking at Blaine's shoulder.

"It's just a graze." Touching the torn coat soaked with his blood, Blaine winced.

"Are you sure? It looks pretty bad. Maybe I should look at it."

"Nae, Cal. It's fine." Blaine wiped dirt off his face, looking back down the trail. "Who the hell was that?"

"My guess? The man who had Lia in the saloon. 'Course, it could be whoever set fire to the barn." Cal continued to watch the area, scratching the short stubble on his chin. "Seems you have more enemies than you realize, boss."

Blaine didn't see how he could. He'd been in Settlers Valley less than three months and knew a handful of people. With this latest threat, he had to consider Cal's words. Glancing at his new ranch hand, Blaine gripped the saddlehorn as a wave of lightheadedness passed through him. Inhaling a deep breath to clear his head, he pushed his hat further down on his head.

"We'd best get going."

Cal nodded. "I'm ready."

Blaine kept his focus on the bull, amazed at how the animal ambled along, oblivious to the gunshot wound along its side. Wishing he felt the same about the shot he'd taken, his grip on the saddlehorn tightened. Sucking in more air, he opened and closed his eyes, trying to still the dizziness. No matter how the wound throbbed, he had to keep going.

"Boss?"

His body swaying in the saddle, Blaine righted himself, giving his head a quick shake.

"Boss? Are you all right?"

Blaine thought he heard a voice through his muddled brain, but couldn't be certain. Sensing someone sidling up beside him, he mumbled something unintelligible before his eyes rolled back, numbness claiming a body already going limp.

"Ah, hell," Cal mumbled, unable to do anything except watch Blaine tumble to the ground.

"Ma'am, can you hear me?" Jedidiah Coates pressed a cold cloth to the back of Lia's head and another to her forehead. "Ma'am?"

He looked at the other two men standing over her. Continuing to press the cloths to her head, he motioned for one to hand him a quilt folded across the end of the sofa. Draping it over her, he touched a hand to her cheek.

"No fever," he muttered to himself.

The two Maidu tribesmen spoke little English. Their contact with white men remained limited after various villages had suffered numerous attacks over the last ten years. Moving their villages farther into the nearby hills, they kept to themselves, venturing out on rare occasions.

A soft moan brought their gazes back to Lia's face.

"Ma'am?"

Eyes opening to slits, she tried to lift her head, groaning at the intense pain. "My head," she groaned again, touching a hand to the lump at the back, as if to emphasize her discomfort. "What happened?"

"You tripped over a rug and hit your head."

As painful as it felt, the corners of her mouth slid upwards. "They won after all."

Jed cocked his head, brow lifting. "Who won?"

"The rugs." Turning her head, she stared at the man kneeling beside her until her eyes focused. "Who are you?"

"Jedidiah Coates, ma'am. Friends call me Jed."

She looked behind him. "And them?"

"These are friends from the Maidu village."

Reaching out her hand, she drew in a breath. "Please, help me sit up."

Holding her hand and placing his other behind her back, Jed assisted her up.

"Thank you." Touching the back of her head again, Lia winced.

"Are you Blaine's wife?"

Her eyes snapped open. "Me? No. I'm just a friend of his from Conviction. I'm Lia Jacobs."

Standing, Jed stepped back. "It's a pleasure to meet you, Miss Jacobs."

"I apologize for being such a poor hostess, Mr. Coates."

"Jed, please. We expected Blaine to be here, so finding a beautiful woman instead is nothing to apologize about."

"I do believe you're teasing me, Jed." Attempting to stand, she grabbed the hand Jed offered, swaying slightly when she got to her feet. "It isn't like me to be so clumsy."

"To be honest, I believe the sight of my two friends startled you. You stepped away, catching your heel on the rug."

"Well, thank you for helping me. May I get you some coffee? Or perhaps whiskey, if I can find some?"

"No, thank you. We would like to wait until Blaine gets back. Do you know how long he'll be?"

"I'm afraid I don't. He and Cal went to fetch a bull Blaine purchased. You're welcome to stay as long as you'd like. I should have enough food for you to stay for supper."

"That's kind of you, ma'am, but—"

Shouts from outside stilled his voice.

"Lia!"

"It's Cal." She held a hand to the back of her head, moving as fast as possible to the door. Before she got there, it burst open, Cal rushing inside with Blaine in his arms.

"He's been shot."

Chapter Twelve

"Follow me." Lia no longer felt the throbbing in her head as she hurried down the hall in front of Cal. She stepped into Blaine's room and ripped back the covers. "Place him in the bed, then help me get him out of his coat." Tossing the coat aside, she tore open the blood-soaked shirt. Studying the wound in his shoulder and turning him to his side to check his back, she turned to Cal. "The bullet is still in there."

"Blaine was certain it was only a graze."

"It isn't. Please get me hot water and rags. And send someone for the doctor." Looking past Cal, she noticed Jed and the two Maidu men standing in the hall.

Jed stepped into the room when Cal left to get what Lia needed. "There isn't a doctor in Settlers Valley. The best they can offer is Dahlia Keach."

Her brows furrowed. "The owner of the boardinghouse?"

"I'm afraid so." Jed stepped aside to let Cal back into the room.

"Here you are." He set the bowl and clean rags on the table.

Dipping a rag into the water, she wrung it out, using it to clean around the wound. "I'll need a knife, and tweezers, if you can find them."

A strangled moan escaped Blaine's lips, his eyelids flickering.

"Blaine?" Lia's soft whisper washed over him, prompting his eyes to open to slits.

"Lia?" His voice was brittle and unsteady

"I'm here, Blaine. There's a bullet lodged in your shoulder. I need to remove it."

Closing his eyes, he nodded. "Do it, lass."

"It's going to hurt. You should drink some whiskey first."

He shook his head. "Nae. Do it now."

"But—"

"Lass, please. Get it over with."

Licking her lips, she touched her hand to his forehead as Cal returned with tweezers and a knife. "He's a little warm. Can you bring me some cool water?"

"I'll get it." Jed left for the kitchen, leaving his two companions to look on as Lia picked up the knife.

She touched Blaine's cheek. "Are you certain you don't want some whiskey?"

His eyes opened to slits once more. "Aye, lass. I'm ready."

"All right." Breathing in and out twice to calm her trembling body, she lifted the knife, stopping when someone tapped her shoulder. Glancing behind her, her gaze landed on a strip of leather one of the Maidu men held toward her. "Thank you. Blaine? Bite down on this."

Recognizing what she held out, he nodded, opening his mouth.

Settling it between his teeth, she focused her attention on the wound. "Ready?"

Blaine swallowed, emitting a shaky breath before nodding.

Leaning down, she began to probe the wound, her skin breaking out in a cool sweat. Holding her breath, she forced herself not to look at Blaine's face. Seeing his pain would do nothing except make her job harder.

As she continued to probe, Blaine sucked in a breath on a loud groan when a sharp pain wracked his body.

"I found it." Lia touched the bullet a second time, eliciting another gut-wrenching groan from Blaine. "I'm sorry, Blaine. I should have it out in another minute." When she heard no response, she glanced at him, relieved to see he'd passed out. Holding the wound open, she inserted the tweezers, biting her lip when it slipped twice. On the third try, it gripped the bullet. Slipping it out, Lia held it in the air.

"Here." Cal handed her a bottle of whiskey. "To disinfect it."

Dropping the bullet into a bowl, she took the bottle, pouring the amber liquid onto the wound. Waiting a moment, she drizzled more into the open hole, grateful Blaine hadn't regained consciousness.

"I'll bandage it as best as possible, but I'm concerned about infection."

"Lia?"

She turned to look at Jed. "Yes?"

140

"One of my friends carries medicine that is excellent for preventing infection." Jed nodded to the Maidu men behind him. "Would you consider allowing him to apply the medicine before you bandage the wound?"

Straightening, she turned to study the Maidu, unsure of how to proceed. She knew nothing of Indian cures, but she did understand how plants could be used to treat many ailments. Her mother used comfrey and Aloe vera, instructing Lia on how to apply them.

"Have you seen them help others?"

Jed nodded. "My wife is Maidu. I've seen her use various plants many times with success."

Cal cleared his throat. "I believe you should let them do what they can, Lia."

Pushing aside her unease, she nodded. "Please ask them to help Blaine in any way they can." Stepping aside, she watched one of the Maidu men move to the bed.

Taking out a leather pouch, he removed a dried leaf, crushing it in his palm. Bending down, he pressed the particles into the wound. Studying his work, he straightened, nodding at Jed.

"You can bandage the wound now." Jed stepped back to let the Maidu walk past him and into the hall. "We will come back to speak with Blaine once he recovers. Would you let him know we stopped by?"

"Of course. It was good to meet you, Jed, and please thank your friend for helping Blaine." She let Cal walk them to the door, feeling an urgency to suture and bandage the wound before Blaine woke up.

Finishing with the wound, she laid a hand on his forehead, relieved when it felt cool to the touch. She knew the next few days would be critical. If he showed the slightest hint of infection, she'd load him into a wagon and drive to Conviction. A pang of guilt rushed through her. She still owed the doctors an explanation for her quick departure. They deserved better after giving her so much of their time and believing in her abilities.

"Do you want me to sit with him for a while?" Cal rested his shoulder against the doorframe, his gaze resting on Blaine.

Lowering herself into a chair, Lia shook her head. "I'll do it. I would appreciate you getting the stew to the men. They must be starving."

"That they are."

Hearing the click of the door closing as Cal left, she clasped her hands together, watching Blaine's chest rise and fall. He'd been lucky the bullet hadn't entered lower, piercing a lung. His odds of survival would've been cut drastically given the small amount of medical knowledge she possessed.

Leaning back in the chair, she found herself wondering about her father and brother. Had they left Conviction? Perhaps they'd given up their search and returned to the farm. Even if her father decided to continue, there'd be no reason for them to travel north.

As they would've learned by now, Lia didn't seek out small towns where she'd be unable to get a job and blend in with the locals.

Conviction had been the smallest to date with a population at least four times Settlers Valley. If Blaine hadn't found her, Lia had no idea how she would've survived.

Conviction

"You're certain the woman you saw matched the description?" Porter Jacobs' gaze bored into the younger man cowering before them.

"I'm certain. She and Warren rode out of town a few days ago, heading north."

"What's north of here?" Orson didn't let his misgivings show. They'd listen to anyone who thought they'd seen his sister, then decide which information held merit.

"Settlers Valley. It's right on the Feather River. I hear the sheriff used to be a deputy here."

Porter stroked his beard. "How large is the town?"

The man chuckled. "Compared to here? Real small. But I understand it's growing due to the jobs at the mine. Lots of men take the steamboat north, hoping to find work."

Orson's dour expression didn't change as the man spoke. His sister had a habit of moving to larger towns, not small settlements with little work. A mine wouldn't entice her, unless...

"What do you know of the man who accompanied her?"

The man scratched his chin. "Let's see. Warren is about thirty, no family I know of, and lives in an old shack outside of town. He's always looking for quick ways to make money."

Orson's brow lifted. "A man who works odd jobs?"

Throwing his head back to laugh, the man shook his head. "A gambler and swindler is more accurate. The talk is your gal must've paid him to take her north. Warren doesn't do anything unless it involves money."

"Are there other towns up that way?" Porter asked.

"North of Settlers Valley, and they're much smaller. If you leave in the morning, it'll take you less than a day to get there."

A grave expression crossed Porter's face. "And you're certain the woman you saw was Permilia?"

"Stake my life on it. She's served me at the Gold Dust many times. But she called herself Lia. You can ask Joe. He owns the restaurant and hotel."

Orson's nostrils flared. "He told us he didn't know a woman fitting her description."

The man tilted his head. "Now that's odd." Looking down the street at the Gold Dust, he shrugged. "Well,

144

I'm telling you, she did and she left town a few days ago. Now, I've told you what I know." He held out his hand.

Porter considered what they'd learned. This was the first time anyone had mentioned his daughter calling herself Lia. She'd preferred the name, but he'd always prohibited her from using it. Making a decision to trust the man, he slipped a hand into his pocket, withdrawing a few coins.

"If you've lied to us, we'll come back through Conviction." Porter dropped the money into the man's hand.

Clutching the coins, he shook his head. "I swear it's the truth, Mr. Jacobs. I'll leave you to decide what you'll do next." Tipping his hat, he dashed off, the money burning his palm.

"He's a gambler, Father. Should we trust him? The last person we believed sent us on a wasted trip to Martinez."

Porter watched the man scurry down the boardwalk and disappear into Buckie's Castle. "You're right about him, Orson. I'm certain he'll have none of the coin left within the hour."

"What of the information he gave us?"

"He mentioned the name she preferred before running off." Bitterness laced Porter's voice.

Orson thought a moment, understanding widening his eyes. "Lia."

"He's the first to mention it to us."

Orson pulled out his pocket watch before glancing up at the sky. "It's too late to start tonight, Father. We should leave at first light."

Instead of the brooding expression Orson expected to see, Porter's eyes brightened, a smile curving his mouth. "We are close, son. Soon, your sister will be returned to our home and justice for her misdeeds will swiftly follow."

Boar's Rock

Lia's head bobbed, eyes slowly opening at loud voices from the entry. A moment later, the door opened, Heather rushing inside.

"Ach, it's true. Blaine was shot." She moved closer to the bed, examining his bandaged shoulder. "How's the lad doing?"

Standing, Lia bent over Blaine, touching his forehead. "There's no fever. He passed out when I removed the bullet and hasn't stirred since."

Caleb moved to stand behind Heather, placing his hands on her waist. "Nate and Geneen are outside talking to Cal about what happened. Was Blaine able to tell you anything?"

Lia shook her head. "No, he didn't say anything about the shooting." She rested her hip against the edge of the bed. "I can't imagine anyone wanting to hurt Blaine or Cal."

"I'd have thought the same until someone burned down his barn." Heather placed a hand on her stomach, moving to stretch her back.

"Sit down, Heather." Caleb grabbed the back of a chair, setting it next to her.

Lia walked to the window, opening it enough to let a cooling breeze cleanse the room. "How did you find out about the shooting?"

Caleb massaged Heather's shoulders, his gaze fixed on Blaine. "Cal sent a rider over. He knew Nate would be back at the ranch for supper. We came right over."

"How is he?" Nate stood in the hall, looking at his friend.

Geneen pushed past him to stand over Blaine. She touched his forehead, a finger skimming down his face, saying nothing as a single tear slid down her cheek. Looking up, her gaze locked on Lia.

"Nate told us you were here. I meant to come by sooner." Brushing the tear away, she stepped next to her. "I'm Geneen, Nate's wife."

"I know. I've heard about you from your family. I'm Permilia Jacobs, but I prefer Lia."

Heather turned to face her. "So you're the lass Blaine has been pining about since moving here."

A slight blush crept up Lia's face. "Oh, I doubt he'd pine for me. We're just friends, nothing more."

Heather snorted. "Ah, lass, you've no idea what you're saying."

Lia's brows scrunched together. Opening her mouth to reply, she closed it at Blaine's moan. Moving to the bed, she bent over him.

"Blaine?" Lia looked at the bandage, seeing no sign of blood. "Blaine, can you hear me?"

His lips parted, eyes opening enough to see her above him.

"Lia," he breathed out.

Taking his hand, the lines of worry on her face softened. "I'm here. How are you feeling?"

"Awful. Do you have water?"

Geneen poured a glass, handing it to Lia. Placing a hand under his head, she lifted Blaine enough to take a sip. When his right hand gripped her wrist, pulling it back for more, she set his head back on the pillow.

"You can only have a sip for now. I'll give you more in a few minutes...if you behave." She heard Heather snicker.

"Who's here?" Blaine shifted, trying to focus on the others.

"All four of us are here, lad." Heather stood, moving so he could see her.

"Cal sent a man to the ranch to get us," Caleb added.

Nate stepped forward. "Do you feel good enough to tell me what happened?"

Blaine sucked in a shaky breath, shifting to get comfortable. "Aye." Licking his lips, he ignored the pain in his left shoulder. "We were bringing the new bull back to the ranch. We'd passed the large rock formation a couple miles from Caleb's place when a shot grazed the bull, then hit the ground." Raising a hand to his mouth, he coughed. "More water, Lia." Taking another sip, he closed his eyes a moment. "He was hiding in the rocks. I'd just drawn my gun when a bullet hit my shoulder. I was able to get to the ground and hide under some bushes. When I saw light flash off his rifle, I fired. I'm certain I hit him." Groaning, he touched his left shoulder.

"Is it hurting?" Lia's eyes showed her concern.

"Aye, lass, but I'm glad you removed the bullet."

Heather's brows lifted. "*You* removed the bullet, Lia?"

Shrugging, Lia looked back at Blaine, whose curious gaze met hers. "I was training with Doctors Vickery and Tilden when, well...when I had to leave Conviction."

"How did you meet the man who brought you here?" Nate asked.

A flash of anger sparked from her eyes before she concealed it. "Through a friend."

"A friend?" Blaine croaked out.

Her face paled at the accusation in his voice.

Heather looked at Caleb, biting back a grin. "I think it's time we rode back home."

"Would you like one of us to stay and help, Lia?"

"Thank you, Geneen, but I'm sure I can take care of him." She cast a look at Blaine, lifting a brow, daring him to argue.

"I would like to ride back tomorrow to see how he's doing."

"And I'll be coming with Geneen. I know what a nuisance the lad can be when he's not feeling well."

Blaine shot Heather an evil glare.

Lia hid a chuckle. "Having you here tomorrow would be wonderful."

Standing, Heather bent down, kissing Blaine's forehead. "You behave, laddie. We'll see you tomorrow."

Blaine waited until they'd all filed out and closed the door before fastening a hard look at Lia.

"We both have plenty of time right now, lass. I want to hear every detail about why you came to Settlers Valley. And you'll not be leaving anything out."

Chapter Thirteen

Settlers Valley

"I have only one room, so you'd have to share a bed." Dahlia crossed her arms, eyes narrowing as she scrutinized the two men standing before her. She didn't need them to tell her they were Mormons, probably from the Salt Lake area. Their clothing, beards, and stoic manner confirmed what she'd suspected when they walked into her boardinghouse.

"That will be fine." The older of the two reached into a pocket, removing coins. After setting them on the counter, he pulled an image out of another pocket, placing it beside the coins. "We are looking for a young woman." He tapped the photograph. "Her name is Permilia Jacobs. She's my daughter. Have you seen her?"

Not one muscle on Dahlia's face moved at the image before her. Some might see her as odd, but her ability to match a girl of perhaps eleven or twelve with the young woman Blaine MacLaren freed from that vile man several days before hadn't diminished.

"Sorry. I haven't seen anyone looking like the picture you have there."

Orson persisted. "She was twelve in the picture. Permilia would be twenty now. Please look again."

Dahlia made a show of picking the picture up, holding it to the light, then setting it down. "I've never seen her. Now, would you like me to show you to your room?"

Porter's features seemed to be cast in stone as he picked up the well-worn image, sliding it back into his pocket. His gaze locked on Dahlia's, as if considering the truth of her statement.

"Yes or no? I haven't got all day." When neither man responded, she set the key on the counter. "Fine. You're in room one at the top of the stairs. I've work to attend to in the kitchen. Supper is at six o'clock."

Picking up her skirts, she held her head high as she pushed open the kitchen door and left their view.

"That woman has seen Permilia."

Letting out a weary breath, Orson shook his head. "She told us she hadn't, Father. Let's put our bags in the room and walk around town. If Permilia is here, someone will know where she's staying."

Porter's jaw tightened, his eyes fastened on the closed door where Dahlia disappeared. "Your sister is here in Settlers Valley."

"How could you possibly know that?"

"I feel her. The Lord has led us here, and we will not be leaving without her."

Orson gripped his father's arm, drawing him outside. "If she's here, we'll find her. And, like always, if this is another misstep, we'll figure out where to go next." The words came out before he could stop them.

He'd never meant anything less. Everything in Orson screamed for them to return home, discontinue their futile search. He knew it imperative he keep most of those thoughts locked inside. His father's wrath extended to everyone, including his oldest son.

Porter came to an abrupt stop. "We should start at the livery. Most everyone stops in there at some point." A strained look crossed his face before his voice boomed, loud enough for any passersby to hear. "And the sheriff. He would keep track of anyone coming into town."

Orson looked up and down the street, unsettled at the outburst. Over the last several months, his father's tantrums had escalated from brief outbursts once or twice a week to almost one every day. Digging fingers into his palm, he scowled.

"Fine. For now, let's put our bags away and eat. Afterward, we'll visit everyone in town who might have seen her."

Dahlia stood at the outside corner of her boardinghouse, waiting until the two men untied their satchels and walked inside. Checking every direction, she straightened, lifting her chin before emerging from her hiding place to walk across the street. Reaching the boardwalk, she increased her pace. Shoving open the door of the jail, she stepped inside, glancing behind her before closing it on a soft click. She jumped at Nate's voice.

"Is someone chasing you, Mrs. Keach?"

Raising a hand to her throat, she shook her head. "Heavens no. However, I do have news for you."

Leaning back in his chair, he rested a hand behind his head. "And what would that be?"

Moving forward, she sat down, leaning toward him. "Two men just took a room at my boardinghouse."

He waited a moment, lifting a brow when she didn't respond. "And?"

"They're looking for that young woman who came into town with that vile fellow a few days ago."

Dropping his arm, his grin slipped away. "Miss Jacobs?"

"Yes, that's the one. The older one claims to be her father. I don't know about the other, but I'm telling you, Sheriff, those two give me the shudders."

Even though the news disturbed him, the corners of Nate's mouth quirked up. "I don't believe I've ever heard of anyone making you shudder, Mrs. Keach."

Straightening her shoulders, Dahlia's eyes lit up. "Yes. It is quite rare." Lowering her voice, she glanced out the window. "I won't let those men hurt that sweet girl."

He chuckled. "You won't?"

She threw up her hands. "Of course not. You have to let Blaine know about them."

Nate thought of his friend, lying in bed with a bullet hole in his shoulder. This wasn't the time for any bad news.

Standing, he grabbed his hat. "I'll let him know, Mrs. Keach. First, you're going to point them out to me. Maybe I'll have a little chat with them before riding out to Boar's Rock."

Stopping him at the door, she grasped his arm. "You aren't going to tell them you know the girl, are you, Sheriff?"

"No, Mrs. Keach, I won't. Are they at the boardinghouse now?" Opening the door, they stepped onto the boardwalk.

"Oh. There they are now, going into Missy's boardinghouse. That girl and her husband serve meals whenever anyone wants." Her mouth drew into a thin line. "I don't know how they do it."

Nate didn't comment. Ever since Percy and Missy Beall opened the boardinghouse a couple weeks before, Dahlia had been grumbling about having competition. With only three rooms, she rarely had a vacancy, leaving travelers to beg for space upstairs in the Lucky Lady or in a few empty bedrooms in personal homes. No one dared bring up the fact to the older widow, not wanting to risk her ire.

"Thank you for coming to see me, Mrs. Keach. I'll go talk to them."

"Don't you think I should come with you, Sheriff?"

Stifling a groan, he shook his head. "I'm sure you have more important work than following me. Besides, we don't want them to know you recognized the girl in the photograph, right?"

"Oh, I hadn't thought of that." Straightening her hat, she gripped her reticule. "I'll expect a full report of what you learn about them. You can never be too careful when it comes to having strangers nosing around in what doesn't concern them."

Biting back a laugh, Nate nodded. "We certainly can't have that, Mrs. Keach." Touching a finger to the brim of his hat, he left her standing outside the jail, already considering what he'd say to the newcomers.

"Sheriff!"

Turning, he stopped when he spotted Josiah Lloyd running toward him, waving a message in his hand. "What is it?"

"A message from the sheriff in Conviction. Said it was urgent." Handing it to Nate, Josiah took a deep breath.

Scanning it quickly, Nate grimaced, his gaze wandering to Missy's. Folding the paper, he stuck it into a pocket.

"Do you want to send a reply, Sheriff?"

"Not now, Josiah. Thanks for getting this to me." Continuing toward Missy's, he thought of Brodie's message, wondering what it all meant, thankful he'd gotten it before speaking with the men.

It wasn't hard to spot the two men eating together, their white shirts and dark trousers held in place with suspenders. Besides, other than the owner, there were no other diners at this time of day. Nodding at Missy, Nate walked to their table.

"Gentlemen."

Porter glanced up, his fork poised a few inches from his mouth. If he or Orson were surprised at Nate's missing left hand, they didn't show it. "Good afternoon, Sheriff."

"I don't believe I've seen you in Settlers Valley. Are you planning to stay or just passing through?"

Setting down the fork, Porter leaned back in his chair. "My son and I are looking for my daughter, Permilia Jacobs. I'm Porter Jacobs and this is Orson."

Nate didn't react to her name as he reached out to shake each man's hand. "And you believe she's here?"

"I do. We heard from a man in Conviction that she and another man traveled this way less than a week ago."

"How old is your daughter, Mr. Porter?"

"Twenty. She's been gone four years. I mean to take her home."

Nate noted the grim determination on Porter's face. "And where is home?"

"We've a farm a few miles from Salt Lake."

Rubbing his chin, Nate cocked his head. "At her age, you might have a pretty hard time getting her to agree to go with you. She might even be married by now."

Porter's face darkened, his eyes turning hard. "She's my daughter and will do as I say."

"Well now, that might be so around Salt Lake. Out here, you'd have difficulty getting anyone to agree with you trying to steal her away. Regardless, I haven't met anyone named Permilia and I know most everyone around Settlers Valley."

A muscle ticked at the corner of Porter's right eye, his mouth twisting in scorn. "If it's all the same to you, Sheriff, Orson and I will stay a few days, enjoy the excellent food and fine company of the people in your town. If there's nothing else?" Porter picked up his fork, indicating the end of their conversation.

"I'll leave you to your food, gentlemen."

Stepping outside, Nate felt a ball of cold fury knot in his gut. The man and his son meant to take Lia back without her consent, using whatever means necessary. He saw it in Porter's eyes, and to a lesser degree in Orson's. Neither seemed to care about her wishes.

Brodie's telegram hadn't been specific about the reasons why the men wanted her to return, but Nate knew his old boss wouldn't have taken the time to send a message if he didn't have grave concerns. It was Brodie's way of warning Nate about an undefined danger. A warning Nate meant to take seriously.

Lia knew Blaine wasn't happy. It wasn't the pain in his shoulder irritating him as much as what she'd done the last twenty-four hours.

Although she hadn't agreed the night before to explain her actions, he'd expected her to comply. Fortunately for her, the pain became so intense, he'd swallowed several mouthfuls of whiskey, not waking until late the next morning. Since then, she'd hurried through checking his bandage and bringing him broth, ignoring his frustrated attempts to get her to stay and talk.

Cooking, cleaning, gathering eggs, and milking the two cows took a lot of time, or so she'd mentioned several times when hastening from his room. She didn't know why it bothered her so much to tell him about the way she'd abandoned her prospective groom, leaving her family and all she'd known. For her, it was a simple decision. Freedom to choose a man she loved, not be forced into a marriage of prestige and convenience for her father.

Lia took both away from him when she fled with a small satchel and even smaller amount of money her mother snuck into her coat pocket. Most times, she felt a degree of freedom and happiness at what she'd done. Other days, she felt the heat of shame.

Without being there, Lia knew her father would've taken out his anger not only on her mother, but on her sisters, as well. As hard as he'd always been, she knew in her heart their punishment for her misdeed would've manifested in a deep, uncontrollable rage lasting days. Her heart ached for what she'd done to them by leaving.

When she did speak to Blaine, the depth of her betrayal to the man her father selected, and her family, would be revealed. As a man who loved his family and valued loyalty beyond all else, Lia shuddered to think of what she'd see on Blaine's face. Disappointment, disgust, pity. Any of those reactions would hurt, especially from him.

"Lia!"

His booming voice reverberated from down the hall at the same time heavy footfalls moved toward the kitchen. Stomach lurching, she gripped the towel in her hands, twisting the material as if it could keep her safe from the wrath moving her way.

Reaching the doorway to the kitchen, Blaine steadied himself against the frame with his right hand, his beleaguered and angry expression pinning her in place.

"Now, Lia. We're going to talk right now, and I'll be hearing no more excuses of why this isn't the time." Letting go of the doorframe, he lurched forward, muttering a curse when he landed against a chair.

Tossing the towel aside, she rushed to him. "You should be in bed."

Shaking his head, he allowed her to help him to the chair. "Nae. This is where I'm meant to be since you've not been staying long enough to finish our conversation." Taking a breath, he leaned his left side against the chair for support, resting his right arm on the table. "It's time you explained everything to me, lass."

Licking her lips, she moved a step away, her gaze moving everywhere except to him. "It's not an interesting story."

The depth of the pain in his shoulder didn't blind him to the fear shuddering through Lia's body. Something had happened, turning the person he saw as a fine, brave woman into someone too scared to face whomever chased her. And he knew, without a doubt, someone was after his woman.

Fletcher, Bram, and probably his brother, Camden, would laugh if they heard such thoughts spoken aloud. Of the lads his age, Blaine had been the one least affected by female flirting. Thanks to Gwen and her days at Buckie's Castle, he knew how to handle himself with a woman, even if his experience had been limited to a few late nights in an upstairs bedroom of the saloon. Not ever had he considered anything more until meeting Lia. Now he thought of little else.

"Sit down, lass. You've delayed long enough, and my temper is too short for you to continue your games."

A shaky hand reached out, pulling the chair away from the table. Lowering herself into the seat, she clasped her hands together in her lap, staring down at them.

"You'll be looking at me, lass." He waited until she raised her head. "Start at the beginning. You've as much time as you need."

Biting her lip so hard she almost broke the skin, she inhaled a slow breath, letting it out in a defeated whoosh.

"First, my family is Mormon."

"Aye, lass. Warren said as much at the Lucky Lady."

"I'm the oldest. My mother is my father's first wife."

His brows lifted. "First wife?"

Misery tinged her features. "My father has four wives. At least that's how many he had when I left. Knowing him, I'm certain he as at least one more by now."

Blaine blew out a low whistle. "That's a fair number of lasses to take care of."

She didn't have to ask what he meant. Living on a farm with a father who had three wives didn't leave much room for privacy. All her siblings knew what happened between a man and woman.

"Yes, well, it's the way of it where I grew up. When I turned seventeen, Father came to me, saying he'd selected my husband. I'd been afraid of the discussion for years. Many girls married at fourteen or fifteen. At seventeen, I thought perhaps I'd be spared..." Her voice trailed off.

"But it didn't happen that way, did it, lass?"

Glancing down, she shook her head.

Reaching across the table, grimacing as pain shot through his left shoulder, Blaine lifted her chin with his finger. "Look at me, lass." When she did, he dropped his hand. "That's better. Tell me the rest."

Dread stilled her breathing as she thought of how to explain why she'd run away.

"Just say it, lass. Whatever is stressing you, we'll work it out. Together."

His words brought the slightest amount of hope, releasing part of the band tightening around her chest.

"The man my father chose for me is a counselor to the president of our ward. He's a respected and wealthy man." She brushed a strand of hair off her face, the light in her eyes dimming even more. "He already has two wives. I would've been his third."

Blaine worked to keep the soaring anger contained. He didn't want to scare her. "How old was he?"

She cocked her head to the side, not meeting his gaze. "At the time, he was in his early fifties, the same as my father."

"And you were seventeen?" He choked out the words.

"Yes," she whispered, the flush of embarrassment coloring her cheeks.

Grinding his teeth, he forced himself to remain calm. "Go on."

"I couldn't go through with it. No matter how much I prayed to accept the man chosen for me, I couldn't do it." She looked up, her eyes filled with pain. "My mother came to me one night with a satchel and some money."

"She helped you escape." It wasn't a question as much as the answer to a prayer.

"I left that night. My father and oldest brother are searching for me. I don't know for how long. They came close to finding me in Sacramento and again in Conviction last week. Cam took me to stay with your family when he heard there were people after me. When I heard they'd left for Martinez, I went back to work at the Gold Dust. The same day, my father and brother returned. I had no choice but to leave."

When Blaine didn't comment, she grabbed the towel off the table, twisting it in her hands. "I know it's hard for you to understand, coming from such a wonderful family. All the MacLarens are so close, so loving, my betrayal must appear a horrible sin."

Blaine's brows lifted, eyes widening. "Sin? I see no sin in you leaving, casting aside the future your father planned. Nae, lass. The sin would've been if you'd stayed, going against your heart and what you felt to be right." Leaning forward, he brushed away a tear streaming down her face. "How did you find Warren?"

Doing her best to stop the moisture in her eyes, she scrubbed both hands down her face. "Carl, Joe's friend, introduced us. Carl had agreed to bring me to Settlers Valley, but he fell out of his wagon, injuring an ankle. Warren was there when it happened. He agreed to bring me—for the right amount of money." She choked out a brittle laugh. "We were robbed when we made camp. They took all my money, everything I'd saved since leaving home. I didn't tell Warren the money had been stolen until we'd reached town." Licking her lips again, she continued to twist the towel, her heart pounding in her chest. "You know the rest."

"Aye." He looked away, his mind working through all she'd said. "Do you think your father and brother will follow you here?"

"I don't see how. Settlers Valley is small, not a town I'd usually hide in. I need a bigger place, like Conviction, where I can find work and lodging." Her nose crinkled before she shook her head. "No. They won't come here. Maybe San Francisco, but not here."

A loud pounding on the front door had her jumping from her chair. "I'll get it." She looked out the front window, seeing Nate with his fist raised, ready to knock again. Pulling the door open, she offered a grim smile. "Hello, Sheriff."

He glanced past her. "Is Blaine in bed?"

"No. He's in the kitchen."

"I need to speak with him." He moved past her, then glanced over his shoulder. "You, too, Lia."

"Nate." Blaine shifted in the chair, looking uncomfortable and in pain. "What brings you out this late? I thought you'd be home for supper by now."

"I would be, except some visitors came to town this afternoon."

Lia's stomach clenched. She reached out, steadying herself against the wall.

"Their name is Jacobs. They've come to take Lia home."

Chapter Fourteen

Lia sucked in a shaky breath, shooting a panicked look at Blaine before placing a hand over her racing heart. "I don't understand how they could've found me."

"They haven't found you yet. Dahlia Keach came to me after they took a room at her place. She recognized you from the picture, but didn't say anything to them. I found them eating at Missy's. Sure enough, they're here to find you."

A trembling hand settled on the back of a chair. Turning it, she sat down, feeling herself pale. "Someone in Conviction must have seen me leave with Warren."

Nate pulled the telegram out of his pocket. "Brodie sent me a message to warn you and Blaine. A man you used to serve at the Gold Dust saw you and Warren leave town. Not long afterward, your father approached him with the photograph. Seems money changed hands. Brodie might never have heard about it, except the man talked about it over several whiskeys at Buckie's." He handed the telegram to Lia.

Reading it over twice, she handed the message to Blaine. "Did they show you the picture?"

Nate nodded. "They did. I told them I'd never seen you before and didn't know anyone named Permilia. Which is true...mostly."

Blaine let out a mumbled curse before setting the paper on the table. "They can't find out she's here."

"Unless someone in town recognizes her from the picture, there's not a chance they'll learn she's with you." Nate glanced at Lia, deciding to go ahead and speak his mind. "If they do learn she's here, living alone with a man, well..." He tilted his head to the side, letting his meaning become clear.

Jumping up, Lia crossed her arms, glaring at Nate. "We've done nothing inappropriate." Her face flushed at the slight fib.

Blaine reached out, wrapping his arm around her waist to pull her close. "He meant nothing by it, lass. Nate's right. The fact you're living with me without another woman as a chaperone reflects on us both. I should've been thinking of that when I brought you here."

Her shoulders relaxed. "You brought me here because you won a wager against Warren. As I recall, you weren't the least bit happy about it, either." A playful grin pulled the corners of her mouth.

"Nae, not at first." He glanced at his bandaged shoulder. "You being here may have saved my life, lass. For that, I'll always be grateful."

The grin slipped from her face. Lia didn't want his gratitude for doing what any decent person would do. An ache tugged at her heart at the realization that what she wanted more than anything was his love.

Nate's fingers drummed on the table. "I doubt many in Settlers Valley care about appearances. It doesn't mean your father will excuse the living arrangements. His disapproval might work in your favor, Lia."

"I might agree with you if he was like most fathers. Unfortunately, he sees me as more of a possession than a daughter. I'm afraid living here with Blaine will do little to change his mind about taking me back. It's a matter of pride for him, you see. Forcing me to return means he won and I've lost. I'm quite certain if I ever return, I'll never be allowed to leave, not even for a trip to town."

She moved away from Blaine, walking to the sink, looking out the window.

Watching from his chair, Blaine's chest squeezed at the desolation on her face. "I'll not let them take you, lass. This can be your home for as long as you want."

"There's more."

Both turned to look at Nate, seeing his serious expression.

"What is it, lad?"

"Before I rode out here, Marcus stopped me. I was in a hurry to get you the news of Lia's father and brother being in town, so I almost didn't stop. I'm glad I did." He leaned forward, resting his arms on the table. "He was in the Lucky Lady last night, playing cards. One of the men at his table was Warren." Nate looked at Lia, seeing her flinch. "What caught Marcus's attention was the way he favored his right arm, hardly moved it. After a time, Marcus noticed a slight stain come through Warren's shirt. He swears it was blood."

Blaine's gaze hardened as he tried to straighten, wincing when the effort tugged at his shoulder. "Do you think Warren shot me?"

"It wouldn't surprise me, not after you won the wager."

Lia stepped toward them. "Blaine offered to pay him what I owed. Warren didn't have to take the wager."

Blaine looked at her, softening his voice. "He wanted *you*, lass, *not* the money. Warren had no intention of letting you go until you paid him in full. Since you had no money, he had no hesitancy about taking what he wanted in trade."

"Blaine figured the man's weakness quickly."

"Gambling..." she breathed out.

"Aye, lass. The lad couldn't pass on an opportunity to make money by accepting my challenge."

Biting her lip, Lia asked the question plaguing her since the day Blaine won the wager, dragging her from the saloon. "What would've happened to me if you hadn't won?"

Using his good arm, he leveraged himself enough to stand, caressing her cheek with his fingers. "You'd have left with no one but me, lass. Only me."

Clearing his voice, Nate stood. "I'm going to ride back home. Tomorrow, I'll do some checking on Warren. Too bad we don't have a doctor in town. If Warren was wounded, he'd have gone there, then we'd have our answer."

Blaine scrubbed a hand down his face. "Aye, but we don't have a doctor."

"We do have Benji at the Lucky Lady and Mrs. Keach. Between the two of them, they know most everything going on in Settlers Valley."

"Wouldn't Mrs. Keach have said something if she suspected anything, Nate?"

"Only if she knew Warren was injured and Blaine had been shot, Lia. I'm not certain she knows either. Doesn't mean I won't speak with her, and Missy Beall. I heard Warren has a room at her boardinghouse." Nate settled his hat on his head. "I'd suggest you don't leave the house, Lia. Blaine, make sure Cal and the others know not to speak about her to anyone. I'll ride back out if I learn anything."

Waiting until Nate left, Blaine reached out his hand, grabbing Lia's and pulling her onto his lap.

"I'll hurt your shoulder." The protest sounded weak, even to Lia.

"Nae, lass. You'll hurt me more by standing too far away. I've been wanting you right here for days." He let his lips trail from her temple to the sensitive spot below her ear, feeling her tremble. Gliding them down her cheek and along her jaw, he captured her mouth, hearing her soft moan.

Breaking the kiss, he buried his face against her throat, wrapping his uninjured arm around her waist and pulling her closer. He lifted his face to claim her mouth again, deepening the kiss this time. Instead of the reluctance he anticipated, she lifted her hands from his shoulders, wrapping them around his neck. Shifting on his lap, she heard a low groan.

"Ah, Lia. You're going to be the death of me," he breathed against her lips. Drawing away, Blaine rested his forehead against hers. "We must stop, lass."

Her brows furrowed, confusion clear in her eyes. "Did I do something wrong?"

A soft chuckle broke from his lips. "Nae, lass. You did everything right, and that's the problem." Seeing her confusion, Blaine tightened his hold for a moment, kissing her once more. "If I had two good arms, I'd already be carrying you to my bed."

Her eyes widened in understanding.

"Aye, lass. It's the way of it between us. Someday..." He let his thoughts trail off, enjoying the flush creeping up her face. Dropping his arm from her waist, he helped her stand, instantly missing the feel of her next to him.

Touching her heated face, she let out a ragged breath. "I should warm our supper."

Blaine watched her move to the stove, her steps a little unsteady. He ached to tell her how he felt, how much he wanted her to stay at Boar's Rock, but now wasn't the time. Blaine had no intention of tying her to him, making her a target before discovering who threatened him. Between the fire and the shooting, at least one person wished him harm. His guess was more than one.

He understood Warren. He'd bested the man at cards, winning a prize both of them coveted. His instincts told him someone different had set fire to the barn. Although there'd been no further threats, he wasn't ready to lessen his guard, putting Lia in further danger. She already had enough weighing on her.

Blaine's protective instincts flared when she'd described the future her father planned. He knew of communities such as this, had heard people talk of them. Lia was the first woman he'd met who had experienced the life. He couldn't imagine any of the MacLaren women accepting such a fate. The idea of anyone telling his sisters or cousins who they'd marry brought a smile to his face.

"I hope this is enough." Lia set down a meal of stew and biscuits. "Cal took most of it out to the men." She glanced behind her at the counter. "I do have some vinegar pie—" She yelped when he tugged her back onto his lap, then laughed when he fumbled with his fork.

"Let me help you." Taking it from his hand, she stabbed a piece of meat, along with a cube of potato, bringing it to his mouth. When he continued to stare at her, she touched it to his lips. "How this works is you have to open your mouth."

Brow raised, a slight grin broke across his face before he let her slide the food into his mouth. His gaze locked on hers, he chewed slowly, feeling the heat build between them. Swallowing, he slid his hand behind her neck, drawing her down for a leisurely kiss. Releasing his hold, Blaine pulled back, noting the dazed look in her eyes.

Lia ran a finger along his chin. "I thought you said we shouldn't be doing this." Standing, she touched his shoulder.

A self-deprecating grin curved the corners of his mouth. "Aye. Seems I can't keep my hands off you."

"Then it may be best for me to keep my distance from you, Blaine MacLaren. You're a dangerous man indeed." Lia bit her lip, looking away, not ready for him to see the danger he presented to her heart.

Settlers Valley

"What's for breakfast, Missy?" Warren picked up a napkin, tucking it into his shirt, his gaze wandering over the boardinghouse owner, ignoring her husband standing less than ten feet away.

"Eggs, ham, and pancakes, Mr. Poe." She kept her distance and her voice low. Missy hadn't wanted to rent him a room when he walked in a few days ago. Needing the money, her husband, Percy, overruled her concerns. He'd regretted the decision after a few short hours.

Warren's gaze continued to move over her. "All of it sounds fine, Missy, along with anything else you'd like to serve with it."

Clearing his throat, Percy stepped next to her, settling a hand on her back. "I'll take his order."

A relieved breath moved past her lips as she turned away.

"Do you have something you want to say to me, Percy?"

He waited until Missy was out of sight, lowering his voice. "You'll get your breakfast, Warren, and nothing more. When you're finished, I want you to pack up and get out."

Warren choked out a feral laugh. "I've no intention of leaving, and I doubt you've the courage to do much about it."

Percy had never been a violent man, avoiding conflict whenever possible. Warren caused his past convictions to flee, the desire to attack the man overwhelming. Anger flaring, he drew back his arm, letting it drop at the sound of the door opening.

"Good morning, Percy." George, Nate's lone deputy, walked inside. "I heard Missy was making her pancakes for breakfast." Pulling out a chair, he sat down several tables away from Warren. "Mrs. Keach isn't happy about me coming over here instead of eating at her place, but..." He shrugged, his eyes twinkling with amusement.

Percy shot Warren a venomous glance before turning back to George. "Dahlia will get over the slight. Even she knows Missy's pancakes are the best in town."

"I do believe you're right. A large helping for me." George settled back in the chair, crossing his arms, watching Warren shift restlessly. Nate had given him specific instructions not to let the man out of his sight. His boss had also given him one more task, one that might not be as easy.

Voices drew his attention to two men coming down the stairs. George knew them as those looking for a runaway young woman. He also knew they'd moved from Mrs. Keach's boardinghouse to stay at Missy's. They'd never spoken to him, although he'd learned the two had visited every establishment in town, showing a picture the older one kept in his pocket.

"Good morning, Porter, Orson." Warren raised his coffee cup toward the men. Their dark expressions skittered over him before they found seats at a nearby table.

Percy walked in from the kitchen, a plate in each hand. "Here's your breakfast, Warren. Remember what I told you." Giving the man a sharp glare, Percy continued toward George. "A couple extra pancakes for you, Deputy. Missy said to let her know if you need more."

"You tell your wife thank you for me."

"I'll do that." He walked to the Jacobs's table, stopping them mid-conversation. "Missy is serving eggs, ham, and pancakes this morning."

Porter spoke first. "I'll have the eggs and ham only, Mr. Beall."

Orson glanced up at him. "I'll have it all, Mr. Beall."

"I'll get your orders to Missy right away."

A few tables away, George ate his meal, lifting his gaze enough to watch both tables. None of the men realized how far sound carried. He could hear every word, even those spoken in a low whisper.

"We've nowhere else to go, Father. Everyone in town has seen the photograph and not a single person recognized her."

"She was young, Orson, and the image is old and worn from showing it for so long." Porter's stern gaze glanced about the room, coming back to his son. "Permilia is here. I can feel it."

George saw the instant Warren's eyes widened, his cup stopping partway to his mouth. He leaned closer to Porter.

"Even if she is, we can't force her back with us. She's no longer a child under your rule."

Porter's face turned a splotchy red, his voice fierce. "She's a willful child, not a woman who can make decisions for herself." The words hissed from him. "Permilia needs strong discipline beyond the law of this town." He paused, breathing through his nose, chest heaving. "Regardless of what the girl wants, we aren't leaving without her."

Chapter Fifteen

"You're certain that's what Mr. Jacobs said?" Nate stood at the window of the jail, looking toward Missy's.

George nodded. "I am. Then they got up and left. Warren walked out a minute later and caught up with them. I followed, but tried not to get close enough for them to get suspicious. The three talked for a bit, the older one showing Warren the photograph, then went their own ways. I don't know what they said, but they seemed to agree on something before they split up."

Nate stepped away from the window, his gut clenching. "Where are they now?"

"Warren went back into Missy's. He came out a few minutes later with his saddlebags and rode north, toward the gold mine." George shuddered at the thought of the Acorn Gold Mine and his brief history working for the owner, Leland Nettles. "I didn't see where the other two men went. Sorry, boss."

He clasped a hand on George's shoulder. "No need to apologize. You did real good." Grabbing his hat, Nate walked to the door. He didn't like knowing one of the few people who knew about Lia and her Mormon background had spoken to her father. "I need you to find Porter and Orson Jacobs. Find me if you get any impression they're leaving town, especially if they turn toward Boar's Rock. If you can't find me, you're to follow them. They cannot get to Blaine's ranch."

George shot a quick look out the window, nodding. "I'll make certain they don't get close to the ranch. It's just..." His brows scrunched together.

"Just?"

"Unless you want me to arrest them, how am I going to stop them?"

A wry smile broke across Nate's face.

George's eyes widened. "You *want* me to arrest them?"

"Long enough so I can get out to Blaine's ranch and warn him. Tell them something's missing from the boardinghouse and they were identified as the men who took it. Hold them for an hour, tell them it was all a mistake, and let them go."

George pulled out his gun, checking the cylinder before shoving it back into the holster. "If I do lock them up, where will I find you?"

"At Marcus Kamm's blacksmith shop. That's where Warren's been boarding his horse. He may have said something to Marcus."

"There's something else about Warren."

"What is it, George?"

"While watching him at breakfast, he favored his right arm. Had a helluva time cutting the ham. I think you're right about him being injured since you first saw him at the Lucky Lady." George watched as Nate's jaw tightened. "Maybe he is the one who shot Blaine."

"I think that's a distinct possibility. Now I need to prove it."

Circle M Ranch

"Where in blazes have you been, lad? You never came home last night and your ma is sick with worry." Ewan MacLaren stood in front of his son, Fletcher, taking in his disheveled appearance, inhaling the strong aroma of whiskey.

Fletcher put a hand to his temple, wincing. "Can you be keeping your voice down a wee bit, Da?"

Ewan had no sympathy for him, staying out all night and coming home drunk. "Eejit," he spat out. "Your ma's been talking of whipping your arse for being a dunderhead and upsetting the laddies and lassies."

Fletcher grimaced, thinking of his younger sister, Kenzie, and the twins, Banner and Clint. By this time, they'd be in the ranch schoolhouse, getting their lessons from Colin's wife, Sarah, or Quinn's wife, Emma.

"'Twas one night, Da."

"One more, lad." Ewan shook his head, remembering the fuss his wife made when Fletcher hadn't arrived by midnight. "I know you've not been handling Sean's leaving well, but the lad had to go. We all knew it was coming and have accepted it. You need to be doing the same."

Scrubbing a hand down his face, Fletcher's bloodshot eyes met his father's. "Aye, Da."

"Since the lad left, you've been seeing the bottom of too many bottles. Cam and Bram have accepted it well." Blowing out a weary breath, Ewan nodded to the stairs. "Get yourself cleaned up. Cam and Bram are training a new colt in the corral. The others are out with the herd."

Massaging the back of his neck, Fletcher started for the stairs.

"The lads mentioned you've been spending time with a girl at Buckie's."

Stopping, he looked over his shoulder. "All the lads spend time with lasses at Buckie's, Da."

"A great deal of time."

Fletcher's face heated. He wasn't going to discuss any woman with his father, and certainly not Maddy. Bram and Camden had done their share of teasing him over the young saloon girl. Even so, he couldn't stay away from her. They'd told him to enjoy her company, nothing more. The MacLarens were open-minded people, to a point. Neither believed Ewan or Lorna would be too accepting of a woman who'd been making a living on her back.

"The lass is of no concern, Da. She means nothing to me." The lie tasted bitter to his tongue. "I'll be down in a bit to help Bram and Cam."

"And you'll be doing less of the drinking, right, lad?"

Gripping the stair railing, he gave a reluctant nod. "Aye, Da."

Shoving open the door to his bedroom, he tossed his hat aside. Lowering himself onto the bed, he rubbed his eyes, hoping to relieve the pounding in his head. He'd lied to his father. Staying away from Maddy, along with the whiskeys accompanying each visit, wouldn't happen.

The week Lia left town, he'd gone into Buckie's Castle with Bram, looking for something. He didn't know what at the time. After a couple glasses of the amber liquid, his gaze locked on a vision coming down the stairs.

A body-hugging, royal blue dress enhanced the golden blonde hair she'd piled high on her head. One hand caressed the banister as she took each step, her gaze searching the room. Leaning one arm on the bar, Fletcher continued to stare, his breath catching when her wandering gaze met his and held. Her mouth opened slightly, a pink tongue gliding out to lick her lips.

"Holy..." Fletcher breathed out, his body tightening at the small gesture.

"What, lad?" Bram shifted toward him, following his gaze. "Ah. A new lass." He set his glass down. "I believe I'll go introduce myself."

Fletcher's arm had shot out, his hand tightening on Bram's. "Nae."

The one word had Bram studying his cousin's face, seeing an expression he'd never witnessed before. When Fletcher's grip tightened, Bram held up his other hand.

"Enough. I've got your message, lad." He settled against the bar, watching the young woman approach.

An almost fragile smile lifted the corners of her mouth. "Good evening, gentlemen."

Bram waited a few seconds. When Fletcher still hadn't spoken, he tipped his hat. "Good evening. I'm Bram MacLaren, and this witless lad is my cousin, Fletcher."

She glanced at Bram, her gaze moving quickly to Fletcher. "Are you?"

He continued to stare, shaking himself when Bram elbowed his side. "Sorry, lass. Am I?"

Her eyes sparked. "Witless."

Straightening to his full six-foot-five height, he noticed her tiny frame for the first time. Swallowing, he tried to get his brain to think, come up with something clever to say. Instead, he shook his head. "Alas, it is one of my biggest faults, lassie."

She cocked a brow. "Lassie? Isn't that a term for a young girl?"

"Or a woman who's small and quite lovely." He ignored Bram's snort beside him, letting his gaze move over her ivory skin until it landed on her startling blue eyes. His mother would've called it robin's egg blue. Fletcher simply thought them the most beautiful eyes he'd ever seen.

A soft chuckle left her lips. "Maddy."

His brows drew together. "Pardon?"

"My name. It's Maddy."

Maddy.

Fletcher scrubbed both hands down his face, shaking his head to rid himself of the memory of the night they met. It had changed everything he'd thought about himself, including his desire to remain single as long as he could.

Pushing up from his bed, he walked to the basin, splashing water on his face. His da was right. He needed to get control, something he hadn't felt since he'd first spotted her.

Changing into a clean shirt, he grabbed his hat, shoving it onto his head before descending the stairs. He needed to prepare himself for another round of mockery from his cousins. They were merciless when it came to Maddy.

He leaned against the corral fence, resting his arms on the top rail, watching as Bram and Camden worked a new horse. A wave of guilt washed over him. Camden should be out with the herd. Instead, he'd taken Fletcher's place when he hadn't returned home.

"It's about time you decided to rejoin the family."

He hadn't noticed them stop and walk over to him, Bram holding the lead line. Fletcher offered no excuse. Only a fierce glare.

"Which of you miscreants told Da about Maddy?"

Holding up both hands, Camden shook his head. "We mentioned a lass. He knows nothing else."

"That would be your decision, Fletch." Bram turned to the colt, running a hand down its neck.

"I'll be saying Uncle Ewan isn't happy with what you've been doing. He and Uncle Ian are up to something, and it can't be good for you, lad."

Fletcher knew they were right. He had responsibilities, jobs needing to be completed. With Caleb and Blaine in Settlers Valley, and Brodie the sheriff, the family was stretched thin and the uncles were growing restless.

The thought of Blaine had him reaching into his back pocket. Pulling out a telegram, he mumbled a string of curses. "Ira gave me this last night to give to Da."

Camden stared at the paper. "What's it say?"

He grimaced. "I've not read it."

Camden took it from him, tearing it open. Reading it, he mumbled an oath before handing it to Bram.

"Ah, hell." He looked up. "The telegram is from Nate."

Fletcher's chest began to squeeze. "Is it Heather, Bram?"

He shook his head. "Nae. It's Blaine. Someone shot him and there's no doctor. A woman is staying at the house to care for him until the wound heals enough for him to get back to work. Do you want to give this to your da, or do you want me to?"

Taking it from Bram's hand, Fletcher read through it, cursing again. "I'll do it."

Camden rubbed a brow. "He's up at my house, talking to Ma."

Stalking away, he headed past his house and Quinn's, seeing no activity. This time of day, everyone would be doing chores, as he should've been doing if he could get his mind off Maddy. This was why he'd never intended to get tied down until he was much older. He didn't need a woman controlling his actions or mind. He never believed it possible until he'd seen the vision in the saloon. After a short time, she governed his every mood.

Kicking at the dirt, he took off his hat, shredding fingers through his hair. Fletcher couldn't blame the lass. She'd never asked anything of him, which should've been a relief. Instead, it brought more guilt, knowing he had no one to blame for his irresponsibility except himself.

Reaching the house where Colin and Camden lived, he bounded up the steps. Opening the door, the sound of women's voices from the kitchen drew him in that direction.

"I'm in here, Fletch." His father's voice had him turning around. He and Ian were in what had once been their brother's study. Angus and their other brother, Gillis, had been murdered a couple years before, leaving a hole in the family no one had been able to fill. Looking between his father and his uncle, Fletcher straightened his back, determined to meet whatever wrath they might bestow on him for his irresponsible actions. First, he had a message to give them.

"Ira gave this to me." He held it out to his father. "It's from Nate."

A grin tilted Ewan's mouth. "I've been hoping for word from the lad." Unfolding it, his grin faded. "Ach. This isn't the news I'd hoped to read." He handed it to Ian.

He read it quickly, his response similar to Ewan's. "We'll need to send someone to help Blaine until the lad is healed." Pinching the bridge of his nose, Ian shook his head. "We've not got enough men to work Circle M, but I see no other way."

Fletcher waited, knowing he should volunteer. He needed to break whatever spell Maddy had cast upon him, put as much space between them as possible. At the same time, the thought of not seeing her for weeks tore a hole in his heart. A reaction he'd never expected.

"The lad has six men. The three we sent, plus the three he hired. They're the lads with experience."

"I say we need a MacLaren there, Ewan. A lad we know and can trust. It'll only be for a couple weeks."

Ewan nodded, frustration evident in the way his shoulders tightened. "The fire and now this. And no doctor in Settlers Valley."

Fletcher cleared his throat. "Nate's telegram says there's a lady taking care of him."

Ian snorted. "Aye. Probably one of the saloon girls who's tended gunshots before."

Fletcher stiffened at his words. He had no doubt his father had told his uncle about a lass in town. According to Camden and Bram, they didn't know anything else about her, including her employer. As much as he believed getting away for a while would help put his head back on straight, he had no intention of causing her any pain.

"I'll go." The words were out of his mouth before he'd thought them through.

Both men turned toward him, his father speaking first. "We've need of you here, Fletch. I thought we could send Thane."

His mouth twisted, brows furrowing at the mention of Bram's younger brother. "He's fifteen, Da."

Ewan glared at him. "Blaine can give him the orders, and Thane will make sure he and the men carry them out. Knowing we've a MacLaren working with the men and the herd is all we need right now."

"There's more to it than watching over the men, Da. What if there's another fire or whoever shot Blaine returns? Thane's too young to carry such a burden."

"He's right, Ewan. Thane will be an excellent rancher in a couple years. For this, we need to send another lad."

Ewan considered Ian's words while studying Fletcher's face.

He said nothing for several minutes, knowing a hasty decision would work against all they'd planned.

"What of the lass, lad?"

His nostrils flared a little before he steadied his gaze. "I told you, the lass means nothing to me. A diversion to keep my mind off Sean."

"Seems a long diversion to me," Ewan countered, crossing his arms.

Gritting his teeth, Fletcher shook his head. "She means nothing to me, Da. I'm the one who should be going. You can't send Cam or Bram with all the new horses needing training. I can leave tomorrow at dawn and be at the ranch early afternoon. Knowing Blaine, he'll send me back within a few days, a week at most."

Ian chuckled. "Aye, the lad's never had much patience."

Standing, Ewan paced to the window. From here, he couldn't see Cam and Bram working the horses down near his house. The rest of the ranch was quiet, everyone overburdened with work needing to be done.

Turning around, he shot a hard look at Fletcher. "One week is all we can spare you."

Nodding, Fletcher felt both relief and dread at the decision. "A week it is. I'll leave in the morning."

Leaving the room, he stopped when Ewan called out.

"Wait a moment and I'll walk with you." He said a few more words to Ian before joining his son. Stepping outside, he placed a hand on his shoulder. "You know, Fletch, of all the lads, you're one of the worst at lying."

"But—"

"Nae. You never could tell a lie with a straight face. As a man, you've gotten a wee bit better, which isn't much." Dropping his hand, Ewan stopped. "You stay with Blaine as long as you need. Get the lass out of your head. We'll be waiting for you when you're ready to return."

Chapter Sixteen

Boar's Rock

"There's the ranch, Father." Orson shifted in the saddle, looking in all directions. At almost noon, he'd expected more activity. "Where is everyone? We heard MacLaren has at least six men working for him."

"As long as she's alone with the man, I don't care where the others are. Permilia won't fight if she believes he's in danger."

Orson's mouth twisted in doubt. "All we know is MacLaren won her in a card game and they knew each other in Conviction. It doesn't mean she has any feelings for the man."

Porter ignored his son, studying the area for a place to hide while they waited. Selecting a group of trees a hundred yards away, he kicked his horse, reining it to a stop when he found the spot he wanted.

"We'll wait for Poe here." Porter dismounted, tossing his reins over a low-hanging branch.

Orson slid to the ground, unease coursing through his body. "I don't trust Warren. Who knows where he rode off to after leaving us or even if he'll go through with what we discussed."

Pulling out a canteen, Porter took a sip. "He's doing this for his own revenge. If Poe doesn't show, we go after her anyway. His plans for MacLaren mean little to me."

Leaning against the trunk of a large oak, Orson slid to the ground, resting his arms on his bent knees. "After all this time, why are we risking so much for a woman who'll run off again?"

"Have you forgotten she's your sister?"

"Of course not," he bit out. "She's willful and stubborn and won't accept her place in a marriage she ran from once. Forcing Permilia to do anything in the past hasn't worked, and I don't see it working now. This isn't going to end well, Father." Orson thought of his own young wife at home, a woman he'd seen little of since their marriage. They'd married for love, a choice his sister hadn't been given.

Porter crossed his arms, glaring at his oldest son. "Are you so ready for your second wife you can't see the need to finish what we started?"

"I've no plans for a second wife."

"Like your sister, you've no choice in the matter. When we return, you'll be taking a second wife, and a third one shortly thereafter."

The ache in Orson's chest worsened at hearing how his future had been arranged. He already knew who his father planned he take for his next two wives. One would be fourteen by the time they returned, the other a young widow of nineteen. Unlike some men, Orson had no desire to be with any woman except his wife and knew taking other women to his bed would kill the love they'd shared since they were children.

He'd used every argument he knew. His father countered each with vague excuses and references to their bible. Though he'd been raised in their church, Orson didn't agree with many of the practices, including plural marriage. Most of the men his age didn't agree, either, refusing to take more than one wife. It was the older members, those his father's age, who clung to the custom, doing their best to force it on their children.

"Even now, the federal government is doing all they can to outlaw polygamous marriages, Father. Why do you continue to force this when our family wants nothing to do with the practice?"

The answer was a hard crack across his cheek. Orson hadn't noticed his father approach, wouldn't have stopped him if he had. He knew this line of talk would cause problems, but he refused to give up his attempts to sway the older man.

"You're still living in my house and will do as I command. It is the son's duty to obey the father, and that's what you'll do." Porter stalked off, his face red, eyes as cold as a blustery Utah morning.

Orson rubbed the spot on his cheek, a new plan formulating. At nineteen, he'd always been the good son, the one who did all his father asked, even if the orders went against his own values. They'd been home several times over the years they'd been searching for Permilia. During the last visit, Orson's wife had implored him to consider leaving. He'd balked, arguing with her until right before riding off with his father once more.

Feeling the sting of his father's hand on his face, Orson reconsidered. If his plan worked, he'd be free of his controlling father, able to begin a new life with his wife. Now to find the courage to put it all in place.

"Stop or you'll burn yourself." Lia swatted at Blaine's hand when he reached for a biscuit. "These are for the men."

"Not all of them, lass." He reached around her other side, swiping one from the pan.

"You must be feeling better if you're in here pestering me. Don't you have work you could be doing in your office?" Using the spatula, she lifted each biscuit from the pan, putting them into a bowl lined with cloth.

Leaning down, he placed a kiss below her ear, then let his lips wander down her neck, gratified at her soft moan. "Aye, there's always work to be done. This is much more satisfying, though."

Laughing, Lia stepped away, feeling her face heat. Each day she stayed created a bigger risk to her heart. Before Blaine, she had no experience with men, only warnings from her mother before stuffing the little money she had into Lia's satchel and telling her to be safe.

The few kisses she and Blaine had shared confused her more than giving her peace. His touch caused her to feel needy, desiring something she couldn't define. She feared they were the same things her father had told her were evil and forbidden.

Catching Lia around the waist, Blaine turned her. "I've wanted to do this all morning." He lowered his mouth to cover hers.

His touch elicited desire, as well as alarm. Blaine had spoken of being careful, not doing what was happening now. Yet at every opportunity he touched, caressed, and kissed her, making it impossible for Lia to make sense of whatever was happening between them. Lifting her hand to his chest, she pushed.

"Blaine?"

Loosening his grip, he looked down at her.

"What are we doing?"

He lifted his brow in uncertainty.

Stepping out of his embrace, she moved to the stove, brushing strands of hair from her face. "You and me. What are we doing?"

Moving behind her, Blaine placed his hands on her waist, but didn't pull her close. "Tell me what you mean, lass."

Inhaling a shaky breath, she blew it out slowly, refusing to turn around. "You tell me we shouldn't be touching or kissing because when we do, it makes it hard not to do more. If that's so, why do you keep doing it? I'm not the same as other women you've been with. I don't understand what's happening."

Dropping his hands from her waist, he stepped away. "I've not been with many women, Lia."

A self-deprecating laugh burst from her lips as she turned toward him. "More than I've been with men."

"Aye." Swallowing, he rubbed the back of his neck, trying to relieve the tension her question caused. Blaine had been trying to figure out the same. Why did he continue to push his attentions on her, doing what he'd said they shouldn't? If he continued letting his desire control him, Blaine knew they'd end up in his bed.

She was nothing like the girls at Buckie's, the only women he'd bedded. Lia was pure and kind, sweet and guileless.

Blaine cared about Lia and enjoyed her company. Did he love her the same as Colin loved Sarah or Quinn loved Emma? He didn't know. Colin had waited years to make Sarah his, and Quinn had known Emma most of his life before figuring out she was the one. Blaine had known Lia a few months.

Glancing up, he saw her watching him, waiting for a few words from him to clear the confusion. "I don't know what to say, lass." Seeing the hurt in her eyes, he wished he could give her more.

Tearing her gaze from his, she returned to the stove, stirring a large pot. "Your wound is healing well."

"Aye, it is."

"If there's no infection, I should be able to return to town in a few days."

"Return?" He moved beside her, noticing the way she refused to look at him.

"Of course, Blaine. I can't stay here." Stirring a few more times, she set the spoon aside, still not meeting his gaze. "I appreciate what you did, getting me away from Warren. I hope what I've done the last few days is enough to repay you."

An emotion he couldn't define gripped his chest, refusing to let go. "I never expected anything from you, lass."

Giving a curt nod, she stepped farther away. "Good, then we're even. As soon as you're able to ride, I'll be out of your way. I'm sure you'd like to get back to the life you had before I disrupted it."

Pushing away the ball of fear building in his gut, Blaine walked around to face her. Touching her chin with a finger, he lifted her face. "You don't have to leave, lass."

Shrugging away, Lia grabbed a towel, wiping her hands. "Yes, I do. I'm used to being on my own and taking care of myself."

"Then work for me. There's no need for you to be leaving if work is what you want."

She wanted so much more than work from Blaine, but Lia refused to voice her need and ruin whatever dignity she still possessed. It would be better to leave than be tormented by his presence every day, worried she'd do something foolish, destroying her chance of a future.

Opening her mouth to respond, Lia snapped it shut at the sound of approaching horses. When she tried to turn away, he gripped her arm, his gaze boring into hers.

"We are not done with this conversation, lass."

Instead of replying, Lia hurried to the front, looking out the window. "Cal and the rest of the men are here." She turned to see Blaine standing a few inches behind her. "I need to finish preparing their supper. *You* need to go lie down. You've been pushing yourself too hard today." Walking past him, she stopped to look over her shoulder. "I'm warning you, Blaine." She pointed a finger at him. "Don't bother me."

Watching her hips sway as she marched from the room, the corners of his mouth slid upward. Blaine might not be certain if he loved Lia, but she wasn't leaving him. Of that he was sure.

"I'm sorry, boss. Mrs. Keach had an emergency at her boardinghouse." George fidgeted with the brim of his hat, unable to meet Nate's eyes. They stood outside the jail, both keeping watch up and down the main street.

Pinching the bridge of his nose, he considered his deputy. "What kind of emergency?"

Fidgeting some more, George glanced up. "A cross belonging to her husband went missing. She was pretty upset. Swore someone had stolen it." He cleared his throat. "I offered to help her look for it before she started accusing anyone. Jacobs and his son were in the general store when Mrs. Keach stopped me on the boardwalk. They must've ridden out of town while I was inside."

"How long have they been gone?"

George's mouth slid down into a frown. "At least three hours. Benji said he saw them ride south, as if riding to Conviction. I tried to find you at the livery, but he said you'd been called to the mine."

Rubbing his eyes, Nate mumbled an oath. "I've got to ride out to Blaine's."

"Wait."

Frustration wrapped around Nate at George's comment. "I can't. They might be—"

George cut him off, nodding over Nate's shoulder. Turning, he spotted Porter, Orson, and Warren entering town, the father and son reining to a stop outside Missy's. Warren stopped beside them, talking with the men for a few minutes before heading on to the livery. Not one of the three noticed the two lawmen standing down the street, watching them.

"They rode in from the direction of Boar's Rock." George crossed his arms, watching while Porter and Orson walked into Missy's.

"They don't have Lia, which means they either didn't find her or something stopped them from taking her."

"What do you want to do, Sheriff?"

Opening the door to the jail, Nate nodded for George to follow him. Once inside, he sat down, rubbing his chin. "We have no choice but to continue watching them. It's clear Porter and his son are determined to take Lia back with them, even if it's against her will. And I believe Warren is after Blaine for besting him at the wager."

George lowered himself into a chair across the desk from Nate. "And you believe he's the one who shot Blaine."

Nate pressed his lips into a firm line. "I do."

Standing, George slapped his hands against his legs. "Then I'll stay the night in the jail and be ready to follow them in the morning."

"I appreciate it. Why don't you get supper? When you're back, I'll head home and ride out to Boar's Rock in the morning. If they do ride out there, they'll have to deal with me."

George walked to the door. "We'll both be there, if that's their intention."

"Fire!"

Lia's eyes popped open, throwing off the covers when the shout came again. She grabbed her wrapper and slipped into it, running down the stairs. Looking out the window, she saw men running around, carrying buckets of water to douse the flames shooting from the new barn. She hurried down the hall and threw open Blaine's door, placing a hand on his arm to wake him.

"There's a fire. You've got to get up." When he didn't stir, she shook his good shoulder, hearing a groan. "Blaine, please. We need to get out of the house."

Worrying when he didn't wake up, she grabbed the pitcher, splashing the water onto his face.

"What the hell?" He pushed up with his good arm, eyes wide. "For the love of God, woman. Are you so mad at me you want me to drown?"

She ignored the question. "You have to get dressed. The barn's on fire."

Tossing aside the covers, Blaine swung his legs to the floor while Lia grabbed his clothes. "Are the lads out there?"

She handed the pants to him, turning around. "Cal has them hauling buckets of water."

"My shirt, lass."

Checking over her shoulder, she faced him, handing him the shirt. "You can't do much with your shoulder."

"I'll do what's needed."

Her eyes narrowed as she bit back a caustic retort. Handing him socks and boots, she looked down at her own bare feet at the same time Blaine noticed what she wore.

"You need shoes and a coat, lass. Go on downstairs, but hurry. I'll meet you outside." When she hesitated, he walked over and grabbed Lia's arms, pulling her forward. Leaning down, he gave her a quick kiss. "Go, lass. I'll be fine."

Nodding, she dashed down the hall and up the stairs. Stopping at the top, she watched Blaine hurry outside, his right hand gripping his left arm to keep it steady. She knew the pain was still great, but he refused to take any of the laudanum Geneen brought with her the day of the shooting. It hadn't been long since Nate had struggled with his own dependence on the drug after losing his left arm below the elbow at the Battle of Brandy Station. It had been a miracle he'd gotten off the drug. Geneen kept it in a locked box, hiding the key where only she knew the location.

"Cal!"

His most experienced ranch hand turned at Blaine's voice. Running over, he took the steps two at a time. "I think we have it under control. Newt was outside when it started. He saw someone running away, but decided stopping the fire was more important."

"The lad was right. Where'd it start?"

"The front right corner is where Newt first saw flames." Cal dragged a hand down his face. "I'd best get back to the men."

"I'll be coming with you."

"No, boss. It'd be best for you to stay here. There's no wind, so we've got it pretty much out. We don't need you doing something to make your injury worse."

Blaine stayed on the steps, not turning when Lia stopped beside him. He wanted to be out there with the men, not standing here like some worthless invalid.

For the hundredth time, he cursed the person who shot him, rendering him useless. Switching his gaze to Lia, his chest squeezed, knowing she planned to leave as soon as he could ride. Her decision left him conflicted.

Blaine needed to heal and get back to work, but he didn't want her to leave. If he could tell her he loved her, the odds were she'd stay. A man of honor, he didn't have it in him to say the words unless he felt them in his heart.

Blaine had some serious thinking to do, and he needed to do it soon.

Chapter Seventeen

Circle M

"You've got all you need, lad?" Ewan stood next to Fletcher as the morning sun barely emerged over the eastern mountains.

Fletcher finished securing the saddlebags before checking the cinch once more. "Aye, Da."

"We can be sending someone else if you've had a change of mind."

"Nae. I'm good with this decision. Blaine needs me, and it will be good to see everyone else."

"And get your mind off a certain lass?"

Fletcher chuckled, although there was no humor in his expression. "I like the lass, Da."

"But?"

Scrubbing a hand down his face, he looked past his father toward the northern hills. "I need to get her out of my head. The lass is taking up too much space."

Ewan tilted his head. "Have you thought maybe the lass is the right one for you?"

An image of Maddy serving whiskey to Buckie's patrons, taking his hand as she led him upstairs, flashed through Fletcher's mind. How could he tell his da about his deep feelings for a saloon girl, knowing there'd be questions he couldn't answer?

"Nae, Da. She's not the right one for me. That's why I must go. You were right telling me to get the lass out of my head."

Clasping a hand on his son's shoulder, Ewan squeezed. "You be safe, lad. As I said before, take what time you need. We'll be all right here until you come home."

"Here you go." Lorna hurried up, a cloth sack in her hand. "You'll not be leaving without food."

Taking it from her, Fletcher's mood lightened. "The ride's not that long, Ma."

"You're a growing boy. What if something happens to Domino?"

Fletcher stroked the neck of his sorrel gelding with a flaxen mane. He had the horse since its birth, been the only one to train him. "Domino will be fine, Ma. I'm still grateful for the food." Leaning down, he kissed her cheek.

Stepping away, she clutched her hands in front of her, lines of worry on her face.

"Don't worry, Ma. I'll be fine."

"I expect a telegram, lad."

"Ma, it's for a week, maybe a little longer."

Draping his arm over his wife's shoulders, Ewan sent a meaningful look at Fletcher. "Send your ma a telegram. We'll be wanting to know how Blaine is doing and hear about the others."

Giving up, Fletcher nodded. "Then I'll be letting you know." Swinging into the saddle, he looked around. He didn't know why this trip felt so different from others. Fletcher knew he'd be coming back. This time, he felt like he was leaving a part of himself behind.

Rolling a heel into Domino's side, he reined north. Reaching the last house, he shifted in the saddle, waving to his father and mother, as well as a few cousins who watched him ride off. A mile later, he cut east, taking the route that would put him on the new MacLaren land. It might take him a little longer, but he wanted to get a sense of the new property while riding along the Boundary River.

He didn't see anyone as he rode the narrow trail. All the ranch hands were south where the herd had been moved for better grazing. Colin, Quinn, and Thane were with them, having no idea their cousin rode north to join Blaine.

Everyone agreed Circle M needed more men. Although many rode west after the war, most had no experience with cattle. Family changes added to the problem. Brodie became sheriff, Caleb and Heather married and left to start Highlander Ranch, Blaine rode off to foreman Boar's Rock, and Sean left for veterinary school.

The departures left little time for those who stayed to train new men. His father and Ian hadn't ridden out with the men in years, handling other ranch business from home or meeting with their banker or attorney in town.

Fletcher had heard them talking the night before, making the decision that one of them would help with the herd each day. The excitement in their voices had lessened his worry about the older men being gone. They might have years on them, but each possessed a vast degree of experience.

By the time he reached the river and the far southern border of Boar's Rock, his body began to relax. Fletcher had spent most of the ride trying to keep his mind off Maddy. When he did think of her, guilt ripped through him. She expected him at Buckie's tonight. He'd given Bram an envelope containing money and a note, obtaining a promise his cousin would deliver it to her when he went to town. Fletcher prayed she wouldn't hate him.

In his mind, they needed a swift break before either developed deep feelings for the other. In truth, he had no idea how Maddy felt about him, other than she looked forward to his visits. The excitement dancing in her eyes each time he walked into Buckie's made the ride worth it.

He'd always been a little cautious, greeting her before going off for a couple drinks and cards at any open table. After an hour, she'd come to stand by his side, placing a hand on his shoulder. Two or three rounds later, he'd excuse himself, taking her hand, letting her lead him upstairs.

He'd visited Buckie's six nights, spending most of his time talking with Maddy, before she'd hesitantly reached out to take his hand. The first time had been awkward, which struck him as strange when he thought about it later. She'd seemed nervous and unsure, her hands shaking as she loosened the tiny buttons on her gown. He'd stepped forward to help, stilling her small hands with his larger ones. If he hadn't known better, Fletcher would've thought the saloon girl had little or no experience.

Watching the trail, he recalled how she'd acted, wishing he'd said something. Afterward, he'd held her, breathing in the scent of roses until they fell asleep. A couple hours before dawn, he'd dressed and kissed her on the forehead before leaving enough money to cover the entire night.

He'd done the same each night after, making sure no other man shared her bed. Over the next several weeks, he'd done the same each night by claiming all her time, making sure no other man shared her bed.

His attention moved to a group of deer grazing by the river's edge, scattering when they spotted him on the trail. "Skittish creatures," he muttered to himself before coming to an abrupt halt.

Skittish was how Maddy acted much of the time before they'd walk upstairs, her gaze jerking from table to table, hands clasped in front of her. Thinking on it now, Fletcher wished he'd spent more time talking to her about matters of importance instead of trivial topics to pass the time. Most nights, Maddy asked him questions, fascinated about the workings of a ranch.

Almost never had Fletcher shown an interest in her life before Conviction.

Glancing behind him at the trail, he felt a sharp pain in the area of his heart. He'd been with her each night, yet had never spent the time to get to know anything about Maddy. And now it might be too late.

He grimaced, remembering the last part of the note he'd given Bram. Fletcher had informed Maddy he wouldn't be returning to Buckie's when he got back to Circle M. He'd given no reason, thanking her for all their good times together.

"You're an eejit, Fletch. A complete dunderhead."

He looked north toward his destination, then south toward Circle M, knowing he didn't have time to return to the ranch and retrieve the message from Bram. He had to get to Boar's Rock and his cousin. No matter what else impacted their lives, family came first.

Grinding his teeth, he felt conflicted by his responsibilities to the ranch and regret at the words he'd written.

Sitting atop Domino by the river's edge, listening to the gentle sounds of the water rushing past, a wave of shame overwhelmed him. Something didn't make sense with the beautiful, sweet girl working in a saloon.

Fletcher had never shied away from the ladies at Buckie's, partaking of a great deal of what they offered. At almost twenty, he had more experience than most of his older cousins, which he'd always found amusing...until now.

Maddy showed little confidence their first couple nights together, growing bolder as he continued to visit. For the first time, Fletcher realized she didn't act like any soiled dove he'd ever met.

Scaring away the birds with a shouted curse, he again called himself an eejit. Nothing about the girl made sense and he'd only now realized it, when it was too late to do anything. Instead, he made a promise to himself to see her the moment he set foot back in Conviction. No matter the time of day, he'd find Maddy and do his best to make up for any hurt he'd caused.

Settlers Valley

"It's almost eleven, Father. Don't you think we should be leaving for Boar's Rock?" Orson sat on a bench outside the boardinghouse, watching his father pace back and forth.

"We're waiting for Warren. He counseled we should arrive close to dinner. The men will be out with the herd, and MacLaren will be sitting securely in his home, unsuspecting of our approach."

"And Permilia?"

Disgust twisted Porter's face. "Your sister won't know what's happening until we have her on your horse and are riding away."

Rubbing his hands into weary eyes, Orson opened them to stare at his father, dumbfounded at what he'd said. "She's been running for over three years. I cannot imagine her coming back without a fight."

"I'm her father. She'll not fight me on this."

Delusional was the word that popped into Orson's mind. He'd seen it in his father before. The older man proceeding when all he knew indicated the falsity of his views. Orson had no doubt his sister would fight with all she had to keep from returning to a home she hated.

"After this long, Permilia will not go willingly."

Porter stepped next to Orson, glaring down at him. "If that is the case, she will receive the appropriate punishment."

Orson had no idea why he continued his attempts to reason with his father. No amount of logic swayed the man or helped him see any view except the one burned into his mind. Added to the humiliation Permilia caused him when she disappeared days before her wedding, the search had become his obsession.

A search which could prove deadly if his sister fought for her freedom. Orson refused to let that happen.

Porter looked toward the livery. "There he is now."

Warren reined to a stop in front of them. "Are you gentlemen ready?"

"We are. Come along, Orson."

Riding out of town, he fell to the back, watching his father and Warren talk. A mile from Boar's Rock, his father glanced behind him, a severe expression on his face. Orson had seen it many times before, and it never failed to make him shudder.

"By the end of the day, we'll be on our way home with your sister."

Orson nodded, lowering his hand to the holster on his right side, patting it for reassurance. His father owned the same gun, as well as a small derringer hidden in his coat pocket. He kept both loaded. At least he usually did. Last night when his father slept, Orson removed the bullets from both guns, as well as the extra ammunition in his saddlebags.

A small smile curved his mouth, fading when he thought of Warren. Orson had no idea how he'd deal with a man so set on killing MacLaren, which meant he wouldn't hesitate to turn his gun on anyone who attempted to prevent him from seeing it through.

Boar's Rock

Lia scooped potatoes and roast beef onto Blaine's plate, setting it aside to prepare her own. As had become their routine, she'd take his to the study where he'd spent the last two days. She'd carry hers to the front porch, sitting in a rocking chair while finishing her meal.

They'd barely spoken since she'd announced her plan to leave once he could ride. It hurt to know he cared so little as to not even try to talk her into staying. She didn't count his one attempt when she'd first told him of her decision. It sounded more obligatory than filled with a true desire for her to stay.

Walking through the living room, she jumped at heavy pounding on the front door. Before she could set the plates down and open it, the door burst open, a very tall, very handsome man stepping inside.

"Fletcher? What on earth are you doing here?"

His jaw dropped open. "Lia?" He walked to her, placing a kiss on her cheek. "Are you the woman helping Blaine?"

Setting down the plates, she nodded. "I am. Is that why you're here?"

"Aye. Nate sent a telegram to my da. He and Uncle Ian decided to send someone to help until he recovers."

She smiled. "And that's you?"

"Aye, it is. Where is the lad?"

"In the study. He refuses to stay in bed any longer." Picking up the plates, she handed them to Fletcher. "Take these with you. One for Blaine and one for you."

"What about you?"

She waved a hand in the air. "I've already eaten. Besides, at this point, he's getting tired of seeing my face."

His brows lifted. "I doubt that, lass."

"It will give you two time to talk. Go on now before the food gets cold. The study is right behind you."

Shrugging, he turned, pushing the door open with his boot. "A fine fix you're in, lad."

"Fletch. What are you doing here, lad?"

She watched, seeing the bright smile on Blaine's face, something she hadn't witnessed in days. Lia continued to stand there until Fletcher set down the plates and closed the door.

Shoulders sagging, she returned to the kitchen, searching for something simple to eat. Opening a canister, Lia pulled out a couple biscuits, spread jam on them, and walked out the back door.

Taking the path to the creek, she took a bite out of one biscuit. She loved spending time by the water, watching small fish linger in eddies, frogs hiding under broad leaves. If she had more time, Lia would follow the creek to the Feather River a quarter of a mile away. The arrival of Fletcher meant her plans had changed.

Even if he couldn't ride yet, Blaine got around on his own, and given enough time, could make his own meals. He no longer needed her.

She had little to pack. After doing the last of the laundry in the morning, she'd ask to borrow a horse with the intent of leaving it at the livery. Lia doubted Blaine would object.

"Lia!"

Turning at Blaine's voice, she sighed, leaving the peace of the creek behind to return to the house. "I'm coming."

Stuffing the last of one biscuit into her mouth, slipping the other into a pocket of her dress, she followed the path. Blaine stood at the back door, his expression bland as he waited for her.

"Seems you made quite an impression on Fletch and the rest of the family." He didn't smile as he watched her walk up the steps, holding the door open as she passed by.

"I'm sure Fletch exaggerates." She continued through the kitchen, stopping when he grabbed her arm. Exhaling a shaky breath, she turned. "What is it you want, Blaine?"

"Fletch says you had a particular friendship with Cam."

Pulling her arm from his grip, she studied his face, seeing what appeared to be a spark of jealousy. Lia chided herself for such a silly thought. The same as all the other MacLarens, Blaine had his pick of available women. She doubted he knew how to spell jealousy, much less feel it.

"Cam is the one who got me out of town when my father and brother showed up. He took me to Circle M and introduced me to your family, making sure I felt welcome. So yes, Cam is a friend." Clutching her hands in front of her, she met his hostile gaze. "You have a wonderful family, Blaine. I'd give anything to have a family such as yours." Turning, she walked toward the stairs, ignoring his call for her to return.

Blaine leaned against the doorframe, knowing he'd been a complete dunce. If he didn't make things right, Lia would leave. The thought scared him more than anything he'd ever faced.

Pushing away from the door, he started to follow when shots broke the glass in the living room window. He dropped to the floor, reaching for a gun that wasn't there. Looking up, he saw Fletcher crouched by the front door, his gun drawn.

"Who the hell is that?" Fletcher hissed, sliding a second gun to Blaine.

"MacLaren! We've come for my daughter. Bring her out now."

Picking up the gun, Blaine cursed. "Lia's father. He's come to take her home."

Chapter Eighteen

"What's happening?" Lia raced down the stairs, oblivious to the danger.

"Get down!" Blaine and Fletcher shouted the warning at the same time as another shot entered the house, hitting the dining room wall. Standing, Blaine grabbed her around the waist, pulling her to the floor.

Keeping a firm hold on her, he hissed into her ear. "I think it's your father."

"My..." Her face paled. "How did he find me?"

Another round of gunfire could be heard, a little farther away this time.

"Put your guns down."

"Is that Nate?" Fletcher crawled to where Blaine and Lia lay on the floor.

"Now, Jacobs!"

Some of the tension left Blaine's body as he rolled off Lia and stood. Wincing, he rubbed his bandaged shoulder before reaching out his hand to help Lia up.

"Let me see it."

"Not now, lass." Blaine brushed past her, picking up the gun he'd dropped when protecting Lia. He and Fletcher stepped outside, seeing Nate and George aiming their guns at three men. Blaine recognized one as Warren.

"Is everyone all right?" Nate slid to the ground, not lowering his weapon.

Blaine moved to the edge of the porch, taking a good look at the men he believed to be Lia's relatives. The older one held a gun in his hand, the younger's face twisted in disgust.

"Aye. They're lucky they missed Lia or they'd not still be on their horses."

"It's good to see you, Nate."

"Fletch." He walked to where Porter sat atop his horse. "Drop the gun, Mr. Jacobs. You, too, Warren."

Porter sneered, his gaze darting to the men on the porch. "I'll not give up my gun, Sheriff."

"You will, or all three of you will be spending even more time in jail."

A mocking grin curled Porter's lips. "Those men are holding my daughter. They have no right to keep her here." He looked at the house. "Permilia!"

Blaine walked down the steps, stopping several feet from Porter's horse. "She'll not be going anywhere with you. Not today and not ever."

"She's my daughter and will do as I say."

"Nae. Lia is a grown woman and will make her own decisions. From what I've heard, the lass wants nothing to do with you or her brother." He shifted his gaze to Warren. "You lost a fair wager. If you've a problem, we'll settle it now." Blaine took a menacing step toward Warren.

"You'll do no such thing, Blaine. Get back on the porch with Fletch before I have to take you to jail, too."

Backing away, he'd made it to the top of the steps when Warren drew a second gun and fired, grazing Blaine on the left arm. A split second later, Fletcher's gun discharged, the shot toppling Warren to the ground.

"Dammit." Nate looked at George as he moved to check Warren. "Keep watch on these two."

"Sure thing, boss." George reined his horse in front of Porter and Orson. He looked at the younger man. "Pull your gun out of its holster and drop it on the ground."

"I didn't do any of the shooting." His protest didn't stop Orson from doing as George asked.

"He's alive." Nate shifted to look at Blaine. "Is Lia in the house?"

"Aye, but I'm not bringing the lass outside with her father here."

Nate's jaw clenched. "George, take those two to jail. I'll be back as soon as I can."

A wry smile curved George's mouth. "With pleasure. Get moving, you two."

Porter pounded a fist against his thigh before holding it in the air. "You've not seen the end of this, MacLaren. I *will* have my daughter back."

"Enough, Jacobs. Start moving." George waved his gun toward the trail.

Not long after they'd vanished down the trail, Lia ran out of the house. She gasped, spotting Blaine's fresh wound. "You're bleeding."

He kept his gaze on the trail, not quite trusting George to get the two men to town.

"He's a good man, Blaine. George will make sure they're in cells before I return." Nate looked down at Warren. "Lia, I could use your help."

"But..." She glanced at Blaine's blood-covered shirt, forgetting her decision to leave.

"It's fine, lass. Help Nate, then you can bandage this up."

Taking several reluctant steps, she joined Nate to stare down at the man who'd caused her greatest humiliation.

"You have to help me, Lia." Warren's strained voice and ashen face softened her disdain for the man.

Kneeling, she quickly checked the wound. "The bullet went straight through your arm. You're lucky, Warren."

His eyes widened. "Lucky?"

A brow lifted. "Fletch is a good shot. If he'd wanted you dead, you would be." She assessed the wound once more before standing. "Can you get him inside, Nate?"

"I believe he can walk just fine. Can't you, Warren?"

Grasping his hand, Nate pulled Warren up, feeling a slight amount of satisfaction at the man's agonized groan.

Blaine's mouth twisted into a sneer. "Back bedroom, Nate." When Lia started to walk past, he grabbed her arm. "I'll be in there with you, lass."

"There's no need. It won't take much time."

Gazing in the direction of the house, he offered a mischievous grin. "Then you'll not have to put up with me for long."

"Stop your bellyaching, Warren." Nate held his arm steady while Lia wrapped the wound.

"You're going to have to change this tomorrow, Nate."

He glanced at Lia, grimacing. "I'll get George to do it."

Blaine leaned over her shoulder, watching as she tied off the bandage. "Do you want Fletch to ride into town with you, Nate?"

"Thanks, but I can handle Warren. Fletch shot him in his gun arm, and I've got his six-shooter. Besides, it would suit me fine if he tried to escape." Nate shot a look of warning at Warren. "It'd make my life easier."

"I'm finished. The bandage should hold fine until tomorrow. You shouldn't try moving your arm for a few days, Warren. I don't want you tearing the sutures." Picking up the cloth she'd used to clean the wound, Lia turned away, crossing the room to the basin of water.

"It's getting late." Nate settled his hat on his head. "I'd best get him back to town."

"I'm sending one of my men with you." When Nate opened his mouth to speak, Blaine held up a hand. "No arguments, lad. I'd never hear the end of it from Geneen if anything happened to you."

"Nothing's going to happen. I have his weapon and he's too weak to try to escape. I appreciate it, but I can do this by myself."

Massaging his neck, Blaine studied Warren, not certain the man wasn't faking much of his pain. "You're the one who drygulched me, aren't you?"

Warren's gaze met his, any sign of pain gone as his lips twisted into a sneer. "I don't know what you're talking about."

Blaine's gut churned at the look on the man's face. "Sorry, lad, but I'm sending one of my men with you."

Nate noted his friend's unyielding expression, accepting any argument would be a waste of time. "Fine. Do it quick, as I want to ride out right away."

"I'll take care of it, Blaine." Lia dashed out of the room before he could object.

Nate watched her go, turning to Blaine. "She's had a tough time of it."

"Aye, she has. You need to know. I'll not let Jacobs take her back with him. She stays here."

"Is that what she wants?"

Pressing his lips together, Blaine cocked his head. "We've yet to settle everything."

Nate put a hand on his shoulder, turning him away from Warren. "Do you plan to marry her?"

Glancing away, Blaine rubbed his chin.

"You've not decided, have you?"

Sucking in a deep breath, he shook his head. "Nae, I've not."

"Given how I almost lost Geneen, I'm not the best man to give advice."

Blaine forced a chuckle. "But you will."

"You've talked about her since coming to Settlers Valley. It was obvious to all of us how much she meant to you, and now that I've met her, it's even more obvious how she feels about you." Nate leaned closer. "If you love her, admit it to yourself. Ask Lia to marry you. Don't miss out on your chance for happiness, Blaine."

Blaine, Fletcher, and Lia stood on the porch, watching Nate and Newt ride off with Warren between them. The decision had been made for Newt to spend the night in town, helping George keep watch on the three men taking up space in the jail.

"I need to tend to your wound, Blaine. Come on inside." Lia didn't wait for an answer before leaving the men outside.

"She's a good lass."

Blaine glanced at his cousin, seeing no hint of desire in his eyes. He didn't know where the jealousy came from, why he thought she might hold some affection for Fletcher or Camden. Shame shot through him at thinking either man would betray his trust.

Clasping his cousin on the shoulder, he nodded. "Aye, lad, she is. Come inside while the lass cleans my wound. You can tell me of the happenings at home."

Joining Lia in the kitchen, they sat down. Blaine held his left arm toward her, his attention on Fletcher. "Any news from Sean?"

"Aye. Father and Ian received a telegram when he reached St. Louis. They expect another when he gets to New York. After that..." Fletcher shrugged.

"Scotland is a long distance away. It's certain Aunt Gail is missing the lad."

Fletcher gave a curt nod, thinking how much he missed his cousin. "Aye. It's what the lad wants. When he returns, he'll not be the same as when he left."

Blaine winced when Lia poured whiskey on his newest wound. "Nae, but think of all the lad will have learned. It's the best veterinary school in the world."

"By the time he's done, Sean will have been gone five years." Fletcher scrubbed a hand down his face. "Who knows the changes we'll see in the lad."

Blaine knew how close the two were, understood Fletcher's distress. "For all we know, the lad will be married with wee bairns when he gets off the steamship in Conviction."

Fletcher's head shot up, eyes filled with horror.

Blaine threw his head back, laughing until tears appeared in his eyes. "Ah, lad. I'm jesting. We both know all Sean's attention will be on his studies. The lad has never had an interest in anything but taking care of animals. Of us all, I'd be wagering Sean might never find a lass and marry."

Chuckling, Fletcher's mouth tipped into a grin. "Aye, it's true enough. Still, we'll be missing the lad the entire time."

"That should do it." Lia stepped away. "Don't get up...either of you. I've supper to serve, then I'm off to bed." She brushed hair from her forehead. "It's been a long day."

Blaine and Fletcher continued catching up while she filled plates, setting them on the table. Taking a seat between the two, she said nothing, listening as Fletcher talked of all the happenings since Blaine left.

"And what of you, Fletch? Have you been frequenting Buckie's as you used to?" Blaine chewed his meal. His gaze focused on his cousin, even as his attention strayed to Lia. She picked at her food, shoulders rigid, expression blank.

Shrugging, Fletcher forked a piece of meat, holding it close to his mouth. "Aye, I'm still visiting the saloon on occasion."

Blaine heard the change in his tone, going from warm and jovial to cautious. "Any new people working there?" He saw something pass across Fletcher's face before it disappeared, replaced with a congenial expression.

"Aye. You know how it is, lad. People come and go." He didn't meet Blaine's interested gaze as he stared down at his food.

Lia kept silent, already knowing they referred to the ladies men shared time with upstairs. On occasion, she'd served drinks at Buckie's when one of the regulars felt ill, never venturing above the first floor. For all the years she'd helped with the births in her family, Lia knew little of what went on in the private bedrooms of the saloon. She did understand the excitement many of the men showed at the arrival of a new woman.

"There's more if either of you are still hungry." Lia stood, taking her plate to the sink.

Fletcher shook his head, leaving part of the food on his plate. "No more for me, lass."

She looked down at the plate. "Did you not like it, Fletch?"

"Nae, lass. The meal was bonny. My appetite isn't as keen as I'd thought."

Standing, Blaine took his plate to the sink. "I could use some whiskey, Fletch. Would you have some with me?"

Pinching the bridge of his nose, Fletcher nodded. "Aye. A drink is exactly what I need."

Conviction

Bram and Camden dismounted down the street from Buckie's, tossing their reins over a rail before walking inside. The place was crowded, the tables full of cowhands playing cards and drinking. A tinny piano filled the room with a rollicking tune, a few men tapping their boots to the rhythm.

Touching the pocket holding Fletcher's message, Bram scanned the room for Maddy. His cousin had said she didn't come down until close to seven. Pulling out his pocket watch, he saw he had at least thirty minutes before she would show.

"You haven't told me why we had to be here tonight, lad." Camden held up his hand, ordering two whiskeys from the bartender. "What couldn't wait until Saturday?"

Bram leaned an arm on the bar, keeping watch on the stairs. "Before Fletch left, he gave me a message for Maddy. I didn't think it right to wait any longer. The lass needs to know his plans."

Camden's brows drew together. "The lad mentioned no plans to me." Picking up his glass, he took a sip, wincing as the first swallow of amber liquid burned down his throat.

Pursing his lips, Bram lifted his chin. "Fletch didn't share the contents. My thought is he wanted her to know of his trip to help Blaine and that he'll be back soon." He glanced at Camden over the rim of his glass. "What else would it say? The lad is possessed by the lovely Miss Maddy."

Chuckling, Camden relaxed against the bar. "Aye. I've never seen Fletch so taken with a lass." His gaze lowered to his glass. "Do you think it's serious between them?"

Frowning, Bram rolled his glass between his fingers. "As serious as it can be with the lad. We all know how much he enjoys the lasses."

"Aye, but he's never ridden to town every night for weeks to see the same one."

Rubbing his chin, Bram thought of the look on Fletcher's face when he'd handed the letter to him. Lines of regret defined his features, guilt showing in his eyes. He'd never seen his cousin so conflicted.

"Would it matter if the lad does have feelings for Maddy?"

Camden shook his head. "Not to me. It could be a problem with Uncle Ewan and Aunt Lorna, her working in a saloon."

"Lia worked here and they accepted her."

"Aye, Bram. But we all know she only served drinks. From what we've seen, Maddy entertains men upstairs. It will not be the same thing as with Lia."

Bram had been in Buckie's a few of the times Maddy walked Fletcher upstairs, knew he'd stayed all night, paying for her favors so other men couldn't be with her. Something settled in his gut, an unease he couldn't define and had no desire to try.

"Ah, there's the lass now." Camden held up his glass, getting Maddy's attention.

Bram noted the broad smile on her face, saw her glance around the room, the joy fading when she didn't see Fletcher. Making her way across the saloon, she stopped in front of them.

"Good evening, gentlemen."

Bram touched the brim of his hat. "Maddy. You're looking as bonny as usual."

A sweet flush crept up her face. "The same as always, Bram." She glanced at the door, then back at the two of them.

"The lad isn't coming tonight, lass." Bram reached into his pocket, handing her the letter. "Fletch asked me to give you this."

Neither Bram nor Camden missed the wary expression when she took it from his hand. Catching her bottom lip between her teeth, Maddy opened it, reading the contents. A slight gasp escaped before she pressed her lips together. Reading it once more, she let out a shaky breath, lifting her chin.

"Thank you for delivering this, Bram."

Unable to miss the moisture building in her eyes, he touched her arm. "What does he say, lass?"

Swallowing, she did her best to push aside the pain. Maddy refused to shed the tears screaming for release, wouldn't let Bram and Camden see the agony the letter caused.

Steeling her features, she folded the letter, slipping it into the bodice of her dress.

"Fletcher isn't coming back."

Chapter Nineteen

Boar's Rock

The howl of a coyote had Lia sitting up, pulling the covers under her chin. She didn't mind the screech owls or any of the other animals that roamed the ranch at night. Coyotes always caused the greatest reaction.

People said they didn't travel in groups. Absently rubbing the scar on her thigh, Lia knew from experience that was a lie. She'd been eight, walking in the field near their house at night when she heard the cries. Pulling her shawl tight, she'd turned to run back to the house. Blocking her path were three coyotes. A panicked scream ripped from her throat an instant before one ran toward her.

Lia remembered rolling into a ball on the ground, her arms in front of her face, hearing several shotgun blasts, each one closer than the last. It hadn't taken Orson long to find her, covered in blood from a jagged laceration on her thigh. Cradling her in his arms, he'd carried Lia back to the house. Their father had stood over her, yelling about the stupid decision to wander off at night. Her mother tended the wound, biting her tongue, giving Lia encouraging glances. It was hard to believe it had been over twelve years since that night. Her father hadn't changed at all.

Pressing her lips together, she scooted back down in her bed, hoping for at least a few hours of sleep. The events of the day continued to roll through her mind, causing a painful knot to form in her stomach.

Glancing at the packed satchel sitting on the floor, she let out a resigned breath. After what happened today, she didn't have much choice except to stay with Blaine a few more days, at least until her father accepted she'd never return to their farm.

When Fletcher had arrived, Lia hoped to ride back to Conviction with him. A few hours later, she'd heard him tell Blaine he might stay for a while, maybe until they drove the herd south to Circle M in a few weeks. She'd now have to make other plans to leave Boar's Rock and Settlers Valley.

Staying with Blaine any longer than necessary wasn't a good idea for either one of them.

A soft knock on the door had her tensing. When it opened, her breath caught, seeing Blaine walk in before closing the door.

Sitting up, her brows lifted, wrinkles forming across her forehead. "What are you doing in here?" The question came out as more of a breathless whisper than the stern hiss she'd planned.

Crossing the room, he stood next to the bed, his piercing green eyes boring into hers. "I wanted to make sure you were all right, lass." Without asking, he sat down, stretching his long legs in front of him.

Leaning back against the headboard, she tugged the covers over her chest, telling herself to relax. "I'll be fine. You're the one who was shot...again."

A soft chuckle escaped his lips as he touched the newest wound. "This one's nothing. I've been hurt worse working with the cattle and horses."

"Well, it happened because I'm here, with you." Biting her lip, she forced out the next words. "I should be leaving, Blaine. Being here is only going to cause you more problems."

Scooting closer, he lifted a hand, running a finger down her cheek. "Nae, lass. I'll not be letting you leave. Not until we know your father and brother have given up."

Disappointment moved through her. Those weren't the words she'd hoped to hear.

He moved his hand behind her head, pulling Lia closer. "After they've given up and left, I want you to stay. As long as you want." Lowering his head, Blaine claimed her lips. The kiss was slow, caressing, producing a soft sigh from Lia.

Raising her hands, she rested them on his shoulders, desire flooding her when he deepened the kiss. Moving her hands to wrap around his neck, her fingers tangled in his hair, holding him close.

Her lips pressed more firmly on his, giving in to the passion building between them, stunned at her own eager response. Heat flooded her as the kiss continued, heart beating wildly in her chest. When his hand moved to cover her stomach through the thin fabric of her gown, Lia realized she'd do whatever he wanted without concern for the consequences.

Instead of continuing, he moved his hand to her waist, a groan escaping her lips when he raised his mouth from hers.

"Ah, lass. The things I want to do to you." His lips brushed across hers as he spoke, increasing the ache between her legs. An ache she didn't understand but needed to ease.

Lifting his head, Blaine lowered her to the bed, his eyes bright with passion. "There'll be no more mention of you leaving—not until we've talked of what is happening between us. Are we agreed, lass?"

It took her a moment for his words to pierce her clouded mind. Lips swollen, body still thrumming from their kiss, she nodded. "Yes, we're agreed." Her heart continuing to pound, she said nothing when he stood and left the room, leaving her body pulsing and mind whirling.

Settlers Valley

Nate took one more sip of his morning coffee, then set the cup down. Grabbing the keys from a hook, he walked to the back, unlocking the cells to let Porter and Orson out.

"I'm warning you, Jacobs. Leave your daughter alone and head back home. She's made her decision." Nate lifted their guns from a drawer, handing them to George. "My deputy is going to ride with you until you're out of the town limits. If you and your son return and go after Lia again, I'll hold you for trial."

Porter crossed his arms, his features twisted in disdain. "You've no right to tell us where we can and cannot be, Sheriff."

"After you shot up his place and threatened him, I have every right to protect them. What I should be doing is keeping you in a cell and letting the circuit judge decide your fate. Blaine isn't just a friend. He's like a brother, as is the man who shot Warren. I can't think of any family I'd rather *not* have against me than the MacLarens." Nate glanced between Porter and Orson, seeing the wide-eyed look of understanding from the younger man.

"He's right, Father. She does not want to come with us. Her life is here now."

Porter said nothing, nor did the look of contempt on his face change. "We leave now, Orson."

"What now?" Orson followed George and his father outside, mounting his horse.

Porter's mouth curled into a sneer, his voice lowering to a whisper. "We ride out a few miles and return for your sister tomorrow."

"You're looking very bonny this morning, lass." Blaine leaned down, kissing her neck, feeling her tremble. Reaching around her, he tried to pluck a hot biscuit from the bowl, getting a slap on the hand for his efforts. "You're a hard woman, Lia."

Giggling, she looked over her shoulder, confirming they were still alone in the kitchen before turning to kiss his lips. "You've no idea, Mr. MacLaren."

"Good morning." Fletcher joined them, still rubbing sleep from his eyes. "Smells good in here. Is there any coffee, lass?"

She poured a cup for him and one for Blaine, setting them on the table. "Breakfast is almost ready. The men have already eaten and left."

"Aye. I asked Cal to send Will and Newt out with the rest of the men early." Blaine's brows furrowed. "I didn't mean for you to get up and fix their breakfast."

She slid the last of the pancakes onto a platter, placing it on the table. "I was already awake when I heard them preparing to leave. It didn't take long to fry bacon and scramble eggs. Those will hold them better than hardtack and jerky."

When she set a platter of eggs and bacon next to the pancakes, Blaine covered her hand with his. "Thank you, lass."

It wasn't the words stirring her blood as much as the look in his eyes. She saw something in them, heat and desire, which made her body hum. Blowing out a shaky breath, Lia drew her hand away, clearing her throat.

"It was nothing."

Fletcher watched the exchange, amusement crinkling the corners of his eyes at the same time his chest squeezed. He wondered if Bram had already delivered his message to Maddy and what her reaction had been. Seeing Blaine and Lia dance around their attraction caused Fletcher's heart to skip. He knew something important was slipping away and he could do nothing about it.

Blaine scooped up a forkful of eggs. "I'd like you to stay at the ranch today, Fletch."

Blinking away his thoughts of Maddy, he nodded. "Aye. It's a wise decision. I don't trust those men to leave." Fletcher glanced at Lia. "We'll not let them take you, lass. Unless you want to go with them."

"No." Her response came with more force than she intended. "I mean, I'd rather stay here."

Fletcher turned his attention to Blaine, a grin turning up the corners of his mouth. "Seems you've charmed the lass."

Blaine's gaze moved to Lia. "No more than she's charmed me."

Heat suffused her face, his words meaning more than she cared to admit.

"Cal said you've some cows in the pasture next to the new bull. It's time to put him with them."

Blaine set down his fork. "I should be out there with you."

Lia sat down next to him. "But your arm?"

"Will be fine, lass. All I'm wanting to do is watch. I'll not be doing the work unless the lads need my help." Blaine shot an amused glance at Fletcher.

His eyes flashed. "I'm thinking you'd be safe sitting on the porch in the rocking chair, lad. Lia could give you some mending to do while the men work." A quick punch in his arm had Fletcher laughing.

Giggling at their antics, Lia picked up their empty plates. "All right, you two. Get out of my kitchen so I can clean up and start the rest of my chores."

"Do you want some help, lass?" Blaine followed her to the sink.

Fletcher stood, walking to the door. "I'll meet you outside, lad."

Blaine waited until she set down the plates before slipping his arm around her waist. Drawing her close, he captured her mouth with his, deepening the kiss when she sighed against his lips. Their kiss continued until he forced himself to pull away and rested his forehead against hers, both breathing hard. Pushing aside the overwhelming desire to linger, he stepped away.

"I'd best get outside before the lads do something foolish." Placing a quick kiss on her nose, he walked out.

The corners of her mouth slid upward when she heard him whistling. Placing a hand on her heaving chest, she bit her lip, forcing herself back to work.

"The man is too great a distraction," Lia murmured to herself, happiness she hadn't felt in a long time lifting her spirits.

"He's not an anxious bull, is he, lad?" Blaine kept his gaze fixed on their new purchase. The animal seemed to have more interest in grazing than the cows scattered around him.

Fletcher stood on one side of him, arms crossed, studying the over two thousand pound animal. "Nae, he isn't. Maybe he's just hungry."

"Or lazy," Cal added from Blaine's other side. "Never saw a bull that didn't have a hankering for a female when the time was right."

"You sure those cows are ready, Fletch?"

Raising a brow, he let out a disgusted snort. "I'd not have put them together if they weren't."

"Maybe he doesn't like an audience."

Blaine and Fletcher whipped their heads toward Cal, who lifted his chin.

"Well, maybe he doesn't. You just don't know about bulls sometimes."

Blaine leaned his good shoulder against the fence, his incredulous expression hidden below his hat. "Have you ever seen a bull that cared about anyone watching, lad?"

"Hell no." Cal scratched his chin. "I've never seen one this disinterested, either."

They watched in silence for several more minutes before Fletcher spoke. "What do you think Lia's da is going to do, Blaine?"

"Wish I knew. When Newt rode back from town, he said Nate planned to have George escort them out of town with a warning not to return. He's keeping Warren in jail until the circuit judge arrives." Rubbing the sore spot on his arm, Blaine shook his head. "They've been after the lass for years. I'm thinking a warning isn't going to keep them away."

"I'm afraid nothing short of taking a bullet is going to change their minds about the lass, Blaine. The look on her da's face wasn't of a man who would give up. Nothing Nate says is going to change his mind."

"Do you want me to keep a couple of the men close to the house, boss?"

Pursing his lips, Blaine rubbed a hand across his brow. "Nae. The lads are needed with the herd. You and Fletch are here and we'll be watching for them."

"If you two don't need me anymore, I'm going to go check on the men."

"We're good, Cal. I'm thinking of moving the herd to the east in a couple days. Take a look at where they're at and let me know what you think."

He nodded at Blaine. "Sure thing, boss."

Fletcher watched him leave before turning back to watching the bull. "He's a good lad. Seems to know more than most cowhands."

"Aye. I'm lucky to have him and his brothers. All three are good, but Cal is the best, and a natural leader. I'll be talking to your da and Uncle Ian about it once this place starts making money."

"Which won't be long. We'll drive your herd down to Circle M in a few weeks. Da told me prices are good, and you've a nice number of cattle. If you don't break even this year, you will next year." A grin tilted the corners of Fletcher's mouth, seeing the bull mount one of the cows. "Appears everything's looking good for you, lad."

Turning away, they started for the house, Blaine catching a whiff of smoke before Lia's scream had both of them breaking into a run.

"Help! Fire!"

Chapter Twenty

"Get the buckets, Fletch. I'm going to find Lia." Holding his injured arm close to his side, Blaine ran around the house, stopping when he saw flames coming from the end of the bunkhouse. His gaze darted around the area. "Lia!"

"I'm here." She hurried toward him, cradling a bucket of water. Getting as close as possible, she tossed the water onto the flames a moment before Fletcher appeared, a bucket in each hand. "He ran that way." Lia pointed toward the creek.

Taking a bucket from Fletcher, Blaine threw it onto the flames. "Who?"

All three ran back to the water trough, filling their buckets again.

"I think whoever started the fire." Holding the bucket with both hands, she returned to the bunkhouse. "A very small man or maybe a boy," she huffed out. "I yelled at him, but he didn't stop."

As they ran back to the trough, Cal rode toward them, a squirming body draped in front of him. "Stop kicking, you scoundrel." He slapped the person on the rump before thrusting him onto the ground. Dismounting, Cal grabbed him by the collar, forcing him to stand. Lia gasped, seeing a boy standing before them. "You take one of those buckets and help put out the fire you started, or I'll tan your backside so hard, you won't sit for a week."

Fletcher tossed his bucket at the boy. "Get started, lad." He rushed back to the barn, grabbing another bucket for himself and one for Cal. It didn't take long for the five of them to extinguish the fire.

"Thank God you saw it when you did, Lia. We'd have lost the entire bunkhouse." Blaine draped an arm over her shoulders, his gaze narrowing on the boy. "Are you the lad who's been setting fire to my place?"

Saying nothing, his chin jutted out, a defiant expression on his face. Unable to hold Blaine's stern gaze, he swallowed, looking at the ground.

Lia took a step toward him. "What's your name?" When he continued to stare at the ground, she grasped his chin between her fingers, lifting his face. "What is your name, young man?"

Bottom lip trembling, he shook his head.

Lia didn't let go of his chin. "Do you have a name?"

"Jamie."

She almost missed the whispered reply. "Jamie, is it?"

He nodded once, feeling her hand drop away.

"How old are you?"

Jaw tightening, he glanced around, his feet shifting in the dirt.

Blaine moved next to Lia. "Don't think about running, lad. You won't get far, and it will be harder on you. Now, answer the lass. How old are you?"

"I don't know."

Blaine leaned closer. "What'd you say, lad?"

Jerking his head up, Jamie glared at him. "I don't know."

Fletcher took a few steps closer. "I say we give the lad to Nate and let him handle this."

A slice of fear shot across Jamie's face before he looked at the ground again, but not before Blaine saw it.

"Nae. The lad stays here so he can work off what he owes for the fires."

"I ain't doing no work for you and you can't make me."

All three men laughed, Lia placing a hand over her mouth to hide her reaction. Controlling his laughter, Fletcher leaned down, inches from Jamie's face.

"Ah, lad, I'm afraid you've no say in the matter. You work, or we take you to Nate and a jail cell."

Chest heaving, Jamie's shoulders slumped. "How long?"

Blaine's brows drew together. "How long, lad?"

"How long do I have to stay here?"

"You've another place to go?"

Jamie looked at Blaine, giving a curt nod.

"And where would that be?"

Jamie sucked in a shaky breath, knowing the people around him wouldn't care where he wanted to be, the same as everyone else. "Circle M Ranch. I need to find Sarah MacLaren."

Blaine ran a hand through his hair, watching Jamie scoop one bite after another into his mouth. He wondered how long it had been since the boy had a decent meal. From the looks of him, a long time. Finishing his third helping, Jamie pushed his plate away, glancing at Lia.

"Thank you."

Her mouth curved into a playful grin. "Are you sure you've had enough?"

"Yes, ma'am. It was real good."

Picking up the plate, Lia sent a meaningful gaze at Blaine. "I need to get a few chores done. I'll leave you two to talk." When Jamie tried to shove his chair from the table, she held it in place. "You and Blaine need to talk, Jamie. I believe there's much you have to tell him."

Waiting until Lia walked out, Blaine rested an arm on the table, keeping the injured one in his lap. "Why are you looking for Sarah?"

Shrugging, Jamie slouched back in the chair. "She was my teacher where I lived in Oregon. Before she left, she said to find her if I ever needed anything."

Blaine stared at him, remembering his sister-in-law and brother talking about the young boy who had no family. He'd begged to go to California with them. Instead, they left him with the minister and his wife in the small Oregon town where Sarah's family had a ranch.

"What about family in Oregon?"

Crossing his arms, Jamie shook his head. "Reverend Olford got sick and died a few months ago. Mrs. Olford decided to live with relatives in Portland."

Blaine's gaze narrowed on him. "She didn't want to take you with her?"

He stared at the table, refusing to look into Blaine's eyes. "I told her I wanted to find Mrs. MacLaren. I ran away the night before we were supposed to leave." He lifted his head, searching for signs of doubt on Blaine's face. Instead, all he saw was concern.

"How'd you get this far? It's a long way to Circle M from where you started."

Jamie's eyes widened. "You know where Circle M is?"

Until now, they'd all been silent about their relationship to Sarah. "Aye, lad. I know it well. Colin, Sarah's husband, is my brother."

Jamie's mouth dropped open, color draining from his face at Blaine's announcement. Heart pounding, he sucked in a deep breath, building his courage.

"Will you take me there?" The pleading look on his face sliced through Blaine's heart.

"Not yet, lad. You've done some things you must make right before I let you near the rest of my family."

"I'm sorry for the fires, but I had to set them."

Leaning back in his chair, Blaine crossed his arms. "*Had* to set them?"

Nodding, Jamie's face turned solemn. "A man paid me to set them. I think he wants to run you off."

Blaine thought about each of the three fires, none big enough to make him consider leaving Boar's Rock. "Sorry, lad. You'll need to come up with a better reason if you want to see Sarah."

Straightening, Jamie slammed a fist on the table. "It's the truth. He paid me, said you were bad and needed to leave."

"And you believed him?"

"I needed money, and he gave me food."

Blaine chuckled. "Not much from the way you cleaned three plates of food." The smile disappeared, replaced by a serious expression. "Who paid you to set the fires, Jamie?"

"I don't know his name."

"Where do you meet him?"

Looking down, his chin almost touched his chest. "He comes to an old shack between here and the mine. It's where I've been living." The last came out in a broken whisper.

"Does it have a roof?"

Jamie shook his head. "Not much of one."

"A stove?"

He shook his head again.

"A cot, blankets?"

Jamie's head jerked up, the defiance he'd shown when getting caught roaring back. "It's got nothing. The roof leaks horrible when it rains. It's cold and wet most of the time. That's why no one goes there." His chin trembled.

Reaching over, Blaine set a hand on Jamie's shoulder. "No need to be worrying about it anymore, lad. From now on, you'll be living here."

South of Settlers Valley

Orson woke from another night on the hard dirt, rubbing his eyes as he turned away from the early morning light. It had been two days since the sheriff released them from their cells, and all he wanted was to forget all about Lia and ride home. The stubborn cuss of a man who was his father refused to leave without her.

He knew pride drove the old man more than any desire to have his daughter back in the fold. Porter Jacobs cared for little except appearances and the knowledge everyone back home knew he ruled his family with an unrestrainable iron fist. The same fist he had no problem using whenever he believed it would serve his purpose.

Scanning the area around them, Orson's gaze landed on the sleeping form of his father. For a brief moment, he wondered if this might be his chance. It would be simple to head straight for home, pack what he needed, and put his wife on the back of his horse, leaving the farm for good.

Lia had done it with a few clothes, leaving on foot in the middle of the night. Orson and his wife had a much better chance of making it than his sister, yet she'd survived alone.

"What disobedience is whirling in your mind?"

He'd been so lost in thought, Orson failed to see his father rise and stand over him. His shoulders sagged, knowing he'd missed another chance to claim the future he desired.

"No disobedience, Father." Standing, he walked to his saddlebags, pulling out a canteen to take a long draw. Sliding it back in place, he turned, stretching his arms over his head.

"We get her today and go home."

The words hit Orson in the gut. He saw no chance of slipping onto MacLaren's ranch to steal her away. An attempt such as his father wanted would be dangerous, and in Orson's mind, futile. Lia had no intention of leaving and would fight every effort they made.

"It is foolhardy to attempt to get her during the day. She has no intention of leaving, and as those men have proven, they will protect her."

"If I can get her to talk to me, she'll see the error in her ways and come with us. They are preventing her from hearing what I have to say." Porter's expression turned more hostile, the cords of his neck rigid. "They may be holding her against her will."

Orson ground his teeth, doing his best to force away his frustration. "I believe Permilia is where she wants to be. Why is it so hard for you to accept her decision?"

Nostrils flaring, Porter took several menacing steps toward Orson. "She is a willful child."

Holding his hands in front of him, palms out, he shook his head. "She's a grown woman who can make her own decisions. If she chooses to stay, there is nothing we can do."

"If she cares about her younger brothers and sisters, Permilia will come with us."

Anger rising at the implied threat, Orson stepped forward. "You will do nothing to hurt the others if she refuses to come with us."

"She doesn't know that," Porter snarled, the look in his eyes almost feral when he brought his gaze up to meet his son's.

A sick feeling grew in Orson's gut. The last time he'd seen the same look on his father's face was moments before he beat one of his sons to the point he'd almost died. Lia and the other children had been forced to watch. If their father threatened something similar, Orson had little doubt his sister would recall how he'd almost crippled their younger brother. Straightening his back, his icy stare met his father's.

"I'll not be a part of intimidating her to return. If she goes back, it's because she chooses to, not because you threaten her with beating one of our brothers."

Porter's eyes took on a deadly gleam. "Who says I was talking about one of your brothers?"

Boar's Rock

"What will Jamie be working on today?" Lia finished cooking the eggs, sliding them onto a plate for Blaine. She knew he'd suffered through a hard night, his moans causing her to leave her room to check on him several times. When he didn't rise with the others, Lia had let him sleep, ignoring Blaine's grumbling when he came downstairs a couple hours later than normal.

"He's with Fletch this morning. Once the lad understands what needs to be done to repair the bunkhouse, Fletch plans to ride out to the herd."

She set the eggs and a slice of ham in front of him. "And you'll keep watch on Jamie."

Picking up a biscuit, his eyes glinted in amusement. "Aye. I don't believe the lad will run, but I'll not be taking any chances. We've a ways to go before he trusts us."

"Yet he came all this way alone, with nothing, to find Circle M. I don't believe it's a coincidence his path brought him to your ranch."

Swallowing a mouthful of eggs, he took a sip of coffee. "It wasn't planned, lass."

Sitting down next to him, she rested her hands on the table. "No, it wasn't. I'm simply saying perhaps it was fate Jamie ended up at Boar's Rock."

Spreading another biscuit with jam, he thought of what Jamie had told him. "I want to find out who paid the lad to set the fires."

"Has he described him to you?"

"Aye, but it could be anyone. Average height, brown hair, not fat and not skinny. Jamie says he always wore a greatcoat, so he doesn't know anything about the man's other clothing. His hat was similar to what all ranch hands wear, and he kept it pulled low so Jamie couldn't see his face." Pushing the chair back a little, he stretched out his legs, crossing them at the ankles. "Including those working at the mine, there must be at least forty men who match the description Jamie gave me."

"Give him time. He might remember something else." Resting against the back of her chair, Lia's lips turned up at the corners. "The advantage of Jamie being here is he won't be setting more fires."

"Nae, but if whoever paid him learns the lad is with us, he might come after him."

Lia tilted her head. "Why?"

Scratching his chin, Blaine's mouth twisted in thought. "To make certain Jamie can't identify him. Even if the lad never saw the man's face, he heard him talk. His voice could give him away."

"Why would anyone want to run you out? Whoever hired Jamie must know you're not the type of man to give up. You're strong, honorable, hardworking, and..." Lia's voice trailed off, her face flushing at what she'd said.

A smile broke cross Blaine's face. "You don't have to stop now, lass."

Looking away, Lia ignored his comment. Sitting forward, she rested her elbows on the table, hands covering her face. "You've had so much trouble, Blaine. The fires, getting shot—twice—and my family threatening you. It's not fair all of this has come down on you."

Reaching across the table, Blaine pulled her hands away before lifting her chin. "Nothing is ever easy, Lia. Not running a ranch or dealing with those who envy success. My family's name can be a great help or make life harder. It's the way of it, lass."

Leaning toward her, he brushed his lips across hers, igniting desire he'd been working hard to keep under control. The feeling of her soft, full lips exploded through him. Breaking the kiss, he gripped her hands, pulling Lia up to stand in front of him. Staring into eyes already bright with passion, the last threads of control left him when she slipped her arms around his neck. Ignoring the pain, he wrapped one arm around her back, the other around her waist as he covered her mouth with his.

Unwilling to step away, he moved his hands to rest on her hips, tugging her snugly against him, groaning at the feeling of her soft curves against his taut body. Deepening the kiss, he rocked against her, his body burning with need.

Raising his mouth, he buried his face against her throat, raining kisses up the ivory column of her neck. Stopping at the sensitive spot below her ear, he lingered, reveling in her scent.

"Ah, lass. I want you," he whispered, his breath ragged and hot against her ear.

Squirming against him, she tried to get closer, tightening her arms around his neck. "I want you, too."

"Blaine, Lia. Where are you?" Fletcher's voice had them jumping apart. Lia straightened her dress, touching a hand to her heated face.

Taking a deep breath, Blaine moved to the door, his features mired in regret when he glanced over his shoulder at Lia.

Chapter Twenty-One

An hour later, Lia's heart hadn't stopped its fierce pounding in her chest. Nor could she forget Blaine's expression as he left the room. She'd seen the regret in his eyes, the downward turn of his mouth, perhaps even disappointment before he'd left to speak with Fletcher.

Lia knew the attraction she felt for Blaine surpassed anything she'd ever experienced. Then again, she'd never had a serious suitor or allowed herself to care about anyone before him. It still surprised her how little it took for her body to react to his presence, his touch. Nothing in her past prepared Lia for the raging desire pulsing through her at the sound of his voice, the stroke of his hand down her cheek.

None of it seemed real, and that was what produced the doubts rolling through her now. When Lia arrived in Settlers Valley, she prayed she'd made the right decision to follow Blaine. He'd never given her any indication he wanted her with him, never talked of any type of future. Still, she hoped the brief friendship they'd forged would work in her favor.

At some point, after finding work and a place to stay, she'd intended to find Blaine. Instead, he'd walked into the saloon, finding her at the mercy of Warren Poe. Although it seemed like hours, it had taken Blaine mere minutes to offer a solution that freed Lia. He'd never explained why he'd done it or how long he would allow her to stay at Boar's Rock.

With Warren in jail and her family most likely on their way back to Utah, the reasons for her being at the ranch no longer existed.

Wiping her damp hands on a towel, Lia leaned against the kitchen sink. As much as she wanted to stay, she knew it wasn't possible. She couldn't mistake the desire in Blaine's eyes, yet that was where it all stopped.

He'd never spoken of anything more permanent, such as love, and certainly not marriage. No matter her own feelings, she refused to work for a man who wanted her as a convenience with no thought of anything more.

For the first time in years, Lia had a future she could control. No more running from town to town, hoping her father and brother had given up their pursuit. She could go anywhere without looking over her shoulder or sleeping with the fear of waking up to see her father hovering over her.

The enthusiasm for her newly discovered freedom dimmed when she thought of the money she'd need to leave. All she'd saved was stolen by the band of thieves on the trail. Blaine provided a bedroom and food in exchange for her preparing meals, cleaning, and doing laundry. He'd never offered a wage, and she'd never asked.

Rubbing a hand across her forehead, Lia knew the time had come to make a decision. She hated the thought of leaving the ranch, not seeing Blaine each morning, every night, and often in between. Her chest squeezed so painfully at the thought of never seeing him again, Lia placed a hand on the counter to steady herself. Taking a deep breath, she squared her shoulders.

This would be one more in a long list of difficult choices she'd made since leaving home. Although none had been as painful as this one.

Accepting what had to come next, she untied the apron, hanging it on a hook for the last time. Looking around, she felt a slight amount of pride in how the kitchen sparkled and all items had a specific spot on shelves or in cupboards. She'd done that for Blaine. After she left, it would be his only reminder of her ever living at the ranch.

Walking into the living room, she looked out the window. Blaine and Fletcher stood next to the fence, their faces somber, as if they were involved in a serious discussion. Turning, she went to the end of the hall, looking out another window to see Jamie, his expression one of deep concentration as he nailed a board in place. Lia placed a hand on her chest, feeling a slight twinge in her heart.

Walking away, she trudged upstairs, legs as heavy as her heart. Reaching her bedroom, Lia took a slow look around, committing everything to memory.

She didn't give herself time to reconsider. Dragging her satchel from under the bed, it took little time to fill it with the few items she owned. After buckling the straps, Lia removed her coat from the wardrobe and grabbed her gloves from the top of the dresser. She felt a bit of regret at not washing the bedding, knowing if she didn't leave now, the little courage she had would vanish.

Sucking in a resigned breath, Lia wrapped a hand around the handles of the satchel, scanning the room once more before heading downstairs. Reaching the bottom, she refused to linger any longer than necessary.

She grabbed her only hat off the hook, pushing it down on her head. Opening the door, she breathed out as she walked across the porch. Blaine and Fletcher stood in the same place as before, still deep in conversation, neither noticing as she took the steps to the ground.

Tightening her grip on the satchel's handle, feeling the dampness in her hands, she continued forward to within a few feet of them. Blaine was the first to turn his gaze to her, his eyes widening at what he saw.

"Lia?" He couldn't force anything more out, his throat closing in dread.

Unable to meet his gaze, she focused her attention on Fletcher. "It's time I went back to town and found a job." Swallowing, she looked at Blaine. "I appreciate all you've done for me, getting me away from Warren and standing up to my family."

Blaine's body stilled. "You appreciate..." Again, his voice caught, the same as his thoughts.

"You've done so much, but it's time for me to get out of your way, let you get back to life before you took on my problems."

Fletcher saw the confusion and disbelief on his cousin's face. "Blaine doesn't consider you a problem, lass."

She nodded, her gaze moving to Blaine. He remained quiet, his piercing green eyes cold, impassive. When he didn't speak, Lia forced herself to continue.

"I'd like to borrow a horse. I'll leave it at the livery."

"A horse?" Blaine ground out.

Lia nodded. "Just to get to town."

Nostrils flaring, Blaine spun away, taking several long strides before stopping. She could see his shoulders stiffen, back flex as he settled fisted hands on his waist. Daring a quick glance at Fletcher, she bristled at the hostility on his face.

"Surely you didn't think I could stay here forever, Fletch."

Shaking his head, he crossed his arms. "That's exactly what I was thinking, lass. I believe Blaine thought the same."

"Remaining his cook, house cleaner, and occasional plaything?"

Blaine whipped around, stalking to within a foot of her, his face turning purple. "*Plaything*? You think that's all you are to me, Lia?"

Her breath caught at his harsh tone. Before she could form a response, she saw Fletcher draw his gun and move in front of her.

Turning to see what caused his cousin's reaction, Blaine drew his own gun, taking Lia by the arm. A second later, she recoiled at the sight of her father and brother riding toward them.

"Get in the house, Lia." Blaine pulled her away. "We'll talk of you leaving another time." Guiding her to the porch steps, he turned his back to her. "Get inside, then find Jamie and keep him with you."

Her throat thickened as her father and brother drew closer, a look of determination on both faces. She stared, her feet rooted in place.

Glancing over his shoulder, seeing Lia still on the porch, Blaine spun toward her. "Go, Lia. Now."

His harsh tone shook her enough to get her moving. Rushing into the house, she slammed the door, running to the back window. Opening it, she stuck her head out. "Jamie."

He must have heard the urgency in her voice because he spun around, running toward her.

"You need to hurry inside. Come through the kitchen door."

He glanced at his unfinished work. "But—"

"Now, Jamie. I'll explain once you get inside."

Taking another look around, he did as she asked, running behind the house and through the kitchen door.

"What's happening?"

She could hear the worry in his voice, see the terror in his wide eyes. Putting a hand on his shoulder, she guided him to a chair. Sitting down next to him, Lia leaned forward.

"There are men out front who want to take me away with them."

His eyes flashed an instant before he jumped up. "We won't let them."

Grabbing his arm before he fled the room, she pulled him back to the chair.

"Blaine and Fletcher are out there. You're to stay in here with me."

Brows furrowing, he fidgeted in her grasp before nodding. "Why do they want you?"

Releasing the hold on his arm, she clasped her hands in her lap. "It's a long story. I'll explain everything once they've left. All right?"

His bottom lip trembling, Jamie nodded once. "Promise?"

"Yes. I promise."

Seeming to accept her word, he crossed his arms, chest heaving. "All right."

Blaine and Fletcher stood almost shoulder to shoulder, waiting as the men approached. Each held six-shooters, ready for whatever the Lia's family planned.

"I didn't think they'd be daft enough to come back."

Blaine gave a curt nod. "Neither did I, but here they are." His grip tightened on the gun as Porter and Orson reined to a stop. "What do you want, Jacobs?"

"The same as before. I want my daughter, Permilia."

"Then we've a problem. The lass doesn't want to go with you, and you've no power to take Lia against her wishes. I'd suggest you turn around and leave before you do something unwise."

"Unwise is keeping my daughter against her will. It's kidnapping, and I'll not allow it."

The muscles in Blaine's jaw twitched. "The lass is free to go whenever she likes." The truth of the statement hurt as much as a punch to his chest, knowing her intentions of a few minutes before. He shook the unwanted thought of losing her aside, vowing to make Lia see reason once her father and brother rode off.

"Then I insist she tell me herself." Porter looked around, his gaze stopping on the broken front window. "Where is she?"

"Safe inside, away from those who mean her harm." Blaine saw the anger flash across Porter's face, the way his hand moved to settle on the butt of his gun.

"I've got the father. You take the brother." Fletcher mumbled the words, making sure he and Blaine were ready for whatever came next.

Porter slowly drew the gun from its holster, resting it on his thigh. "I won't leave until Permilia tells me it's her decision to stay."

"The lass wants nothing to do with you or your plan to return her to Utah. She's built her own life, Jacobs, and you'll not be stopping her from living it."

Cringing at the sound of the door opening behind him, Blaine risked a quick glance, groaning at what he saw. Lia stepped onto the porch, a shotgun in her hands.

"Stay inside, lass," he called over his shoulder, hoping she'd do as he asked. Instead, he heard her move forward.

"I won't hide inside the house, Blaine." She hadn't reached the railing before her father shouted.

"Permilia."

Holding the shotgun in front of her, she lifted her chin. "Hello, Father, Orson. You've come a long way."

"Stay where you are, Jacobs," Blaine shouted when Porter's horse moved forward, relieved when the older man stopped.

"We're here to take you home."

"I'd think by now you would understand I have no intention of going with you."

"Your place is with your mother. She's not well and needs you."

Lia saw the brief look of disbelief in Orson's expression, the slight shake of his head when he met her gaze. Growing up, her brother had never been able to hide his thoughts or his protective instincts when it came to her. She hoped he still felt the same.

"Mother has done fine without me, Father. As long as you do nothing to hurt her, I'm sure she'll continue to be all right." She paused a moment, as if deciding what more to say. "How many wives do you have now? Six, seven? If anyone has made Mother's life miserable, it's you."

Porter's face reddened, eyes bulging from his head. "You'll not disrespect me, Permilia."

She lifted her chin. "And I'll not leave with you. You've wasted enough years tracking me. Go home, Father, and forget about me."

His angry expression changed, replaced with an icy stare and feral twist of his mouth. "Do you remember what happened to your brother?"

Her chest began to tighten. "I have many brothers."

"This one you'll remember. He refused to do what I asked and hid in the barn." Porter saw the recognition in her eyes. "Do you remember what happened to him when he was discovered?" When she didn't respond, his expression grew more venomous. "No? Then I'll remind you as the same will happen again if you do not return with us."

"No, Father." Everyone's gaze turned to Orson, who'd inched his horse closer to Porter's.

Sneering at his son, he returned his attention to Lia. "Be quiet."

"I'll not be quiet, and you'll not be threatening her. She's made her choice clear to us. We need to respect it and leave."

Lia's heart stuttered in her chest at his defense of her. Of everyone, he and her mother were the only people she truly missed.

"You'll hold your tongue."

"I'll not hold my tongue any longer, Father. Everything she says is true. Your cruel ways and foul temper destroyed our mother and hurt our family. I'll not have you treating Permilia the way you've treated the others. She'll not marry a man forty years her senior."

Blaine's shoulders tightened, disgust knotting his stomach. Lia had told him of her father's plan, but hearing it from Orson made it much more real.

"She's my daughter and will do as I command. If you are not with me, then you are against me."

Blaine and Fletcher saw the instant Porter's finger touched the trigger of his six-shooter. A split second later, he raised the weapon, firing at his son the same time two other shots rang out. A moment passed as the hateful gleam in Porter's eyes changed to disbelief when he looked down, spotting his blood-soaked shirt. He had no time to grab the saddlehorn before toppling to the ground.

"Orson!" Lia ran down the steps, ignoring Porter as she knelt next to her brother. Seeing the blood, she tore at her skirt, panic rising as she pulled at the fabric.

"Here, lass." Blaine knelt beside her, pressing his shirt against Orson's wound.

Tears streamed down her face. "He can't die. Please, help me."

Ripping open Orson's shirt, Blaine studied the wound. "I think it went straight through his side, lass. Look." He nodded, drawing her attention to where the bullet entered, then shifted Orson enough for her to see where it passed through. "Fletch. Help me get him inside."

"I can help, too." Jamie ran toward them.

"Get hot water and towels, lad. Fletch and I will carry him inside."

Nodding, Jamie ran back inside, an anxious Lia refusing to budge from Orson's side. Seeing her grief, Blaine gripped her shoulders.

"You need to focus on what needs to be done, lass. Can you do that?"

Swiping tears from her face, she glanced down at Orson's prone form. "Yes, I can do that."

"All right then. Ready, Fletch?"

At his cousin's nod, they picked up Orson, carrying him into the house. Placing him on the bed, the men stepped back, giving Lia room to examine his wound.

"I'll need whiskey, a needle, and thread." Her voice shifted from the panic Blaine heard outside to the calm, confident woman he wanted to see.

Fletcher left the room, gathering what she needed. Returning, he set the supplies next to the bed, watching as she and Blaine cut away Orson's shirt.

"Will he be all right?"

Looking down, Fletcher saw Jamie by his side, his face ashen.

"If anyone can help him, it's Lia. All we can do is wait and pray. Come with me, lad. They'll not be needing us hovering over them while they work." He grasped Jamie's shoulder, guiding him from the room. "Yell if you need anything."

When they left, Lia looked up from wiping away the blood from Orson's side. "My father?"

Blaine met her gaze, shaking his head. "He's gone, lass. I'm sorry."

Not responding, she focused on her brother. The man she could still save.

Chapter Twenty-Two

Over Blaine's objections, Lia refused to leave her brother's side for two days and nights. Eating little and going without sleep, her strength began to fade. Desperate, Blaine asked Fletcher to ride to Highlander Ranch.

Early morning on the third day, Heather and Geneen arrived, ordering Blaine to get Lia to bed. Lifting the reluctant woman into his arms, he carried her upstairs. Tossing back the covers, he placed her on the bed, cupping her face with his palm.

"Geneen and Heather will look after him, lass. You've done all you can for now."

"I should be the one with him, Blaine." Her weak protest gave him hope she might sleep, maybe even eat once she woke up.

He opened his mouth to respond, closing it when her eyes closed and he heard the soft sound of her gentle breathing. Sitting on the bed, he brushed strands of hair from her forehead, letting his fingers linger a few moments before tracing a path down her cheek. Staring at her peaceful face, he let out a shaky breath.

"I'll not be letting you leave me, lass." He whispered the words, not wanting to wake her.

Blaine didn't know when it happened or why he hadn't realized it sooner. He loved Lia. Had from the moment she'd helped him to her room at the Gold Dust when he was too drunk to walk. She'd never scolded him for his behavior. Instead, she'd slipped from the room. It had been days later when he found himself wondering where she'd slept that night. So many questions. But they had plenty of time. All he had to do was convince her to stay.

Heather and Geneen took turns watching over Orson and changing his bandages, allowing Lia much needed sleep. While one stayed in the room, the other prepared meals and did some of the cleaning.

Blaine had sent Will to Highlander Ranch the evening Porter died. Nate and Caleb had returned to Boar's Rock with him, surprised the two men had been foolish enough to try taking Lia again. They'd loaded Porter into a wagon so Nate could take him to the undertaker while Orson fought for his life.

"The lad has a fever, Heather. Could you bring cool water and a cloth?"

"Aye. Then I'll see to fixing dinner. Fletch said they've been getting by on what he and Blaine fixed." Standing, she moved toward the door.

Geneen lifted a brow. "Now, that must be interesting. From what Nate said, before Lia came to stay at the ranch, Blaine and the men survived on warmed beans and hardtack."

Heather stopped at the door. "Do you think the lass is planning to stay?"

Pressing her lips together, Geneen drew the covers under Orson's chin. "You know as much as me. If she does leave, I'm afraid it will affect Blaine much more than he'll let on. I think he cares a great deal about her."

"Aye, he does. I'm not certain the lad is ready to admit it to himself, though. I'd best get the water and cloth."

A minute after Heather left the room, Blaine walked in, his features drawn, body sluggish as he pulled a chair next to the bed.

"How's the lad doing?"

"He's too warm. Heather is getting cool water. Hopefully, we can get the fever to come down before it goes any higher. How is Lia?"

He scrubbed both hands down his weary face. "Asleep."

Heather returned with what Geneen needed, setting them down on a table by the bed. "What do you plan to do about the lass, Blaine?"

Her question caught him by surprise. "Do with her?" Standing, he motioned for her to sit down.

"Aye. I was thinking you brought the lass here for protection. Nate says Warren Poe is in jail waiting for the circuit court judge, her father's dead, and her brother is wounded. When he heals and rides out, what are your plans for Lia?"

Blaine had known the meaning of Heather's question when she'd asked, stalling for time in order to offer an answer that made sense. How could he explain his thoughts to Heather when he didn't understand the extent of his feelings for Lia?

Leaning against the dresser, he shook his head. "I don't know."

"I'm thinking the lass will leave once her brother has healed. With her father dead, maybe she'll be thinking of returning home."

His jaw tightened as his lips drew into a thin line. He'd stayed awake much of the previous night, wondering the same, trying to come up with a reason for her to stay.

"Aye, she might."

Crossing her arms, Heather glared at him. "And you'll be letting her go?"

Straightening, he returned her hard stare. "I don't have time for this. I'm going outside to help Fletch."

"You'll have to make time for it soon, Blaine. The lad is going to heal, and you'll need to make a decision." Heather's voice softened. "Do you love the lass?"

Closing his eyes, he thought of how she'd dug her way into his life. Lia had become the first person he wanted to see and talk to in the morning, the last face he wanted to see at night. He lay awake thinking about her every night, a smile tugging at the corners of his mouth when he recalled all she'd done for him and the sunshine she brought into his life. From the moment he woke until falling asleep, the urge to touch and hold her overpowered him, wrecking his ability to think. He needed her, wanted Lia in his life, and not for a few days or weeks. Blaine wanted her forever.

A grim expression crossed his face before he gave a curt nod. "Aye. I love her."

Standing, Heather stepped next to him, placing a hand on his arm. "Then you've got to tell her. Don't miss your chance for happiness and let the lass get away."

Those words haunted him over the next few days. Heather and Geneen stayed one night, leaving when Orson's fever vanished and there'd been no sign of infection. Although her brother grew stronger each day, Lia stayed close, unwilling to leave his side for too long.

After a week, and against her protests, Orson forced himself out of bed while she worked in the kitchen. Wincing in pain, he walked to the window, watching a young boy clean out the chicken coop. A grin spread across his face, remembering all the times he and Lia had done the same.

"What are you doing?" She set a tray next to the bed.

"I need to get home, let everyone know of Father's death." He let out a breath, shrugging. "And I miss my wife. I've been gone much too long."

Lia placed a hand on his back. "On a search meant to fail from the first day you left the farm."

He didn't turn toward her, continuing to watch the boy outside. "Father never listened to anyone except the voices in his mind. He believed he could force you to return. As the years passed, he continued to believe the same. In his mind, you were still a young girl under his control."

"I was seventeen when I left, Orson."

He shifted to look at her. "Father always saw you as a girl who needed a firm hand. When you ran off, he saw it as the ultimate betrayal."

She choked out a bitter laugh. "The ultimate betrayal was him bringing more wives into the house, breaking our mother's heart."

He scowled, the veins in his neck pulsing. "Mother was never the same after he married his second wife."

"I'm sorry if this offends you, Orson, but I hated him. I didn't wish him dead, but I feel no remorse, either." She moved when he began to walk past her to the bed. "Will you be taking another wife?"

He whipped around, groaning at the ache in his side. "No." His firm voice left no room for doubt. "I'd already told Father I wouldn't accept another wife. I would've left the farm if he persisted to push me on it." Lowering himself to the bed, his brows drew together. "Why don't you come home with me? Father is gone. You'll be able to choose your own husband."

An image of Blaine crossed her mind before she shoved it aside. He hadn't asked to speak about her decision to leave before her father died and Orson was shot. The satchel remained packed, sitting next to her bed. As always, Blaine had been pleasant and kind. Still, there'd been nothing in his manner suggesting he cared for her more than as a friend.

She touched fingers to her forehead. "I, well...I don't know."

"You'd be loved and needed back home. What are your prospects here?"

As much as she wanted to pretend otherwise, Lia had no prospects and no job. She loved Blaine, but he'd never indicated the same feelings for her. He knew she planned to leave, yet hadn't asked to speak with her, try to convince her otherwise.

Lifting a hand, she tugged on her bottom lip, a habit Lia thought she'd outgrown as a child.

"I won't be healed enough to ride for a few more days. Think about coming back with me."

MacLaren.

Lia rolled the name over in her mind. A strong name for a strong man from a formidable family. He could have any woman he wanted. A profound sadness washed over her, accepting she'd never be the one he chose.

"You may be right. Perhaps it's time for me to return."

Blaine's wounds healed completely over the next few days. With the threats to Lia gone, he'd been able to ride out to the herd with Cal and Fletcher, putting in a long day before returning home. Each night, he'd planned to speak with Lia, but one or the other had been too exhausted for the serious conversation he anticipated.

Two weeks after Orson took a bullet in the side, he decided the time had come to leave. To his relief, Lia had made her own decision to return home with him. They'd stood in the living room soon after dawn, watching Blaine and Fletcher leave with the rest of the men.

"Did you tell him you'll be leaving with me?"

Biting her lip, she shook her head. Glancing at Orson, she saw the disappointment in his eyes.

"You should've told him. He's been good to you."

"Did you tell him about leaving?"

He nodded. "Last night after supper, I mentioned I'd be leaving in a couple days. I didn't say anything about you coming with me." Orson pursed his lips. "Well, there's no time for it now. I'll saddle the horses while you get your belongings."

A numbing sadness claimed her as she walked up the stairs and into her room. Orson was right. She should've talked to Blaine last night, told him of her decision. If she had, maybe he would've protested as he'd done before, given her a reason to stay. Now it was too late.

Picking up the satchel, she placed the last of her meager possessions inside. As she'd done two weeks before, Lia looked around, a sharp pain piercing her heart. Placing a hand on her chest, she pressed hard, doing her best to dispel the anguish of never seeing Blaine again.

"Are you ready?"

She made her way downstairs, meeting Orson at the bottom. "Yes, I'm ready."

"Are you certain about this? If you want to stay, I'll understand."

She'd been asking herself the same, always coming up with the same answer. "Yes, I'm sure."

Taking the bag from her hand, he opened the front door. "Then it's time we left."

Riding at a clipped pace back to the ranch, Blaine cursed himself for leaving the extra rope in the barn. He'd thought of it not ten minutes before leaving, yet still forgot it. He blamed Lia on the lapse.

Orson had said he'd be leaving in the next couple days, which meant Lia might consider going with him. He couldn't allow that to happen. They needed to talk, and tonight might be his last opportunity.

Rounding the last bend, his heart stopped at what he saw. Orson and Lia were on their horses, ready to ride out. Increasing his pace, Blaine told himself she wasn't leaving, only going as far as the ranch's border. His jaw clenched when he spotted the satchel.

Racing forward, he reined Galath to a stop in front of their horses, his chest squeezing so he couldn't breathe. Dismounting, he glanced between them, his gaze locked on Lia.

"What are you doing?"

Gripping the reins so tight her knuckles turned white, she winced at the hurt etched on his face. "I'm leaving with Orson."

"Without telling me?" His eyes took on a cold glint as both hands fisted at his sides. "Do I mean so little to you?"

Mouth falling open, the color drained from her face. "No, that isn't it at all."

He took a couple steps closer. "Then why, lass?"

Lia felt the moisture gather in her eyes. She'd never seen Blaine so shaken and confused. Raising a trembling hand to her face, she swiped away the tears before they could fall.

He dropped Galath's reins, moving close enough to place a hand on her thigh. "Talk to me, lass." Seeing the tears she worked to hide, he raised his arms toward her, lifting Lia out of the saddle to slide down his body. Leaning down, he kissed her forehead. "Tell me why you're leaving," he whispered, feeling her shudder in his arms.

"I can't stay."

"I don't understand."

Ignoring the knot in her chest, she swallowed, regret thick as she looked into his eyes. "I love you. It's too hard living here, knowing you don't feel the same."

A relieved breath broke from his lips. Bending down, he kissed her lips, hearing a cough of censure from Orson. "I do love you, lass. I've loved you from the moment you rescued me from a drunken stupor." Seeing the doubt in her eyes, he kissed her again, uncaring what her brother might think. "Why do you think I brought you to Boar's Rock?"

Her brows furrowed. "To save me from Warren?"

He shook his head. "To save you for me."

Lia's face paled for an instant before a hesitant smile curved the corners of her mouth. "You brought me here for you?"

Blaine took a step back, taking her hands in his. "Ah, lass. Don't you understand? You're who I want beside me, always. I thought I'd lost you once when the uncles sent me to Settlers Valley. I'll not be losing you a second time. I love you, Lia. Marry me. Be the most important part of my future."

An almost strangled cry broke from her lips before she flung herself at him, wrapping her arms around his neck. Hearing his soft chuckle, she drew back.

"Is that a yes, lassie?"

"Always, yes."

His arm wrapped around Lia's waist, they waved goodbye to Orson. When he disappeared down the trail, Blaine turned her to face him.

Lia's heart melted. Each time his gaze met hers, he owned another part of her. Reaching up, she cupped his cheek before settling her mouth on his. A low groan was her only warning before he scooped her into his arms, carrying her into the house, up the stairs, and into his bedroom.

Setting her down, he caressed her face in feather-light kisses before claiming her mouth. Desire surged, erasing the fear controlling him when he'd seen her ready to ride out of his life. Deepening the kiss, his tongue slid across her lips, a groan of pleasure escaping when she opened to him.

He'd never tasted anything so sweet, so pure, so right. She melted against him, pressing her soft curves against his taut muscles. Needing her closer, he tightened his hold, drawing her close, angling his head to deepen the kiss.

His hands slid down her body, pulling up the hem of her skirt, feeling the heat of her as they wandered up her soft skin. His control dwindling, Blaine broke the kiss, raining kisses along her jaw to her ear.

"I want you, Lia. Right here." His chest squeezed as he waited for her response, feeling her body begin to shake.

"Yes, I want you, too. But..." Unable to meet his gaze, her voice trailed off.

Lifting her chin, he stared into her eyes. "But what, lass?"

"You'll have to show me what to do."

Chuckling, he once again lifted her into his arms, carrying her to his bed. "I'll teach you what I know. We'll learn the rest together."

A loud pounding on Blaine's bedroom door drew them out of their lethargic sleep.

"Blaine. Are you in there, lad?"

"Fletcher," he groaned against Lia's neck, kissing the soft spot below her ear.

The sound of the handle turning preceded more pounding. "Blaine, if you're in there, you'd best answer me or I'll kick the door down."

Leaning up on one elbow, he swept the covers back. "I'm in here, you miscreant. What's so urgent?" Sliding into his pants, he stalked to the door, opening it just enough to peer out.

"Cal and I came back when you didn't return. We can't find Lia. Is she, uh..." Fletcher tried to look around him.

Blaine shoved him back before stepping into the hall and closing the door, ready to land a blow to Fletcher's jaw when he saw the knowing grin on his face.

"The lass is in there, isn't she?"

He glanced behind him, unable to hide his satisfied grin. "Aye. She, uh...the lass agreed to marry me." The moment the words were out of his mouth, Blaine knew what he wanted to do. "Get Cal and saddle my horse and Lia's. We're heading to town."

Fletcher's eyes widened. "Now?"

"Aye. We'll be down in a few minutes."

Opening the door, he closed it on a soft click, walking to the bed. Sitting down, he brushed strands of hair off her forehead, leaned down, and kissed her. It was meant to be light and quick, but when her arms wrapped around his neck, pulling him close, neither could resist the instant passion. Minutes passed before he finally drew away.

"You need to get up and dress, lass. We've somewhere to go."

She covered her mouth to stifle a yawn. "Go? Where?"

"It's a surprise. One I hope you'll like." He watched her eyes open wide before she stretched her arms above her head, arching her body toward him. Stifling a groan, he took her hands, pulling her up. "We leave in ten minutes."

Two hours later, they stood inside the church in Settlers Valley. They'd stopped to get Heather, Geneen, and Caleb, then ridden to the jail to get Nate. Oddly, not one commented when Blaine asked them to follow.

It wasn't until they'd reined to a stop outside the church that Lia turned to him, a radiant smile lighting her face. Helping her to the ground, he grabbed her hand, leading them all inside. It had taken five minutes to convince the reverend of their sincere intentions. Thirty minutes later, he slipped a slim gold band on Lia's finger.

"Mr. Blaine MacLaren, you may now kiss your beautiful bride."

He needed no further encouragement, sweeping her into his arms to the sounds of cheers and applause.

Settling her on the floor, he bent once more to kiss her lips. "I love you, Lia MacLaren."

A soft smile curled her lips. "I love you, too. More than you know."

Epilogue

One month later...

"Bring them around this way, Blaine." Colin pointed to where he wanted his brother to merge his and Caleb's cattle with the larger MacLaren herd. Seeing Blaine nod, Colin reined Chieftain around and headed toward the wagon at the back of the herd. Recognizing the occupants, he waved.

"It's about time you came out to meet us, lad. We wondered if we were going to drive the herd to Sacramento by ourselves." Heather laughed when he slid off his horse, put his arms around her waist, and set her on the ground. "Careful, lad. The bairn."

He looked his cousin up and down, a broad smile on his face. "I know of the bairn, lass. You look good. How do you feel?"

She let out a breath. "Better now that we're here."

Looking over her shoulder, he reached out for Geneen. Setting her down, he drew her into a hug. "Sarah is excited to see you. She's missed you, lass." His smile broadened at the sight of his new sister-in-law. "Lia." Walking around to the other side of the wagon, he settled his hands on her waist, placing her on the ground before drawing her in for a hug. "So you got my miscreant brother to settle down." He kissed her cheek, chuckling at the shout behind him.

"Hey. Let my woman go, lad." Blaine rode up to them and dismounted, a grin tipping up his mouth. Clasping his brother on the shoulder, he pulled Lia to him. "I understand you've already met my wife."

Colin nodded. "Aye. She stayed with the family for a bit. Then we heard she'd traveled to Settlers Valley. A coincidence, don't you think?"

Blaine grinned. "Aye. The best coincidence of my life." He shot a look at Lia. "And the best wager I ever made." He looked behind him at the row of houses, one for each of the original MacLaren families. Seeing Jamie sitting on his horse, away from everyone else, he motioned him over. "I've someone for you to meet."

Colin's brows drew together as he watched the boy nudge his horse forward. "Who is this?"

Waiting until Jamie slid to the ground, Blaine put his arm around the young boy's shoulders. "Colin, this is Jamie. He came all the way from Oregon to find you and Sarah."

Colin's jaw dropped. Kneeling, he opened his arms wide. "Jamie."

The boy ran to him, engulfed in Colin's strong embrace. "I came to find you." His voice broke, his small body trembling.

"I know, lad." He pulled back, looking at the boy he'd last seen when he and Sarah left for California. "We talk about you often."

Jamie's eyes widened. "You do?"

"Aye. We wondered how you were doing, how much you had grown."

Jamie's chest puffed out. "I'm much bigger now."

Chuckling, Colin nodded. "Aye, you are." Looking up, he saw Sarah and several others approach. As she got closer, he stood, turning Jamie toward her.

Sarah blinked a couple times before her jaw gaped open. "Jamie," she breathed out, hurrying forward to close the distance between them.

Jamie ran to Sarah, wrapping his arms around her waist. "Please, don't send me back." Tears streamed down his face. "I promise I won't cause any trouble."

Kneeling, she took him into her arms. "I don't know the whole story yet, but if this is where you want to be, we won't send you back."

The other MacLarens gathered around, welcoming their family back, greeting Blaine's wife. Most had met Lia before. All expressed surprise at how they'd found each other. Lia and Blaine laughed, promising to share their story over supper.

Fletcher said his hellos, then milled about, a sense of detachment surrounding him. He'd never felt alone with his huge family and didn't know what to make of the matter now.

"Fletch. It's good to have you back." Bram hugged him. "You are back, right?"

"Aye. Once we get the cattle to market, I'll be coming back here." He looked past Bram to see Camden walking toward them.

"Fletch. Thought you might have abandoned us, lad." He hugged Fletcher. "It's good we're all riding to Sacramento. It will give us time to catch up."

Nodding, Fletcher found himself scanning the crowd, knowing he wouldn't see the person he most wanted to find.

"You'll be telling us of the women in Settlers Valley, right?" Camden asked, clasping him on the shoulder.

"It will be a short discussion, lad. The only women I know are Heather, Geneen, and Lia."

Dropping his arm, Camden laughed. "Ach, that can't be. You're the one we rely on to draw all the lasses to us."

Shrugging, Fletcher shoved his hands into his pockets, looking at Bram. "Did you give her the message?"

"Aye."

"And?"

Bram let out a breath. "The lass didn't seem happy, but she didn't cuss your name, either."

Camden moved forward, keeping his voice low. "I know she worked at the saloon, but the lass seemed to be a real lady, Fletch. Whatever you wrote, she took it hard. The lass tried to hide it, but..."

Bram nodded. "Cam's right. Pain flashed across her face, then it was gone. She folded the message, we talked a few more minutes, and that was it."

Sucking in a deep breath, Fletcher let the familiar pang of guilt wash over him. He experienced it each time he thought of Maddy and the message he'd given Bram to deliver.

"I'd best go see her tonight before we leave in the morning."

"Nae, lad. It will do no good."

Fletcher looked at Bram, brows furrowed. "She's so mad she won't see me?"

Bram shook his head, his gaze shifting to Camden before returning to Fletcher. "The lass is gone. She left Buckie's Castle."

Thank you for taking the time to read Blaine's Wager. If you enjoyed it, please consider telling your friends or posting a short review. Word of mouth is an author's best friend and much appreciated.

Watch for book eight in the MacLaren's of Boundary Mountain series, Fletcher's Pride.

Please join my reader's group to be notified of my New Releases at:

https://www.shirleendavies.com/contact-me.html

I care about quality, so if you find something in error, please contact me via email at

shirleen@shirleendavies.com

About the Author

Shirleen Davies writes romance—historical and contemporary western romance with a touch of suspense. She is the best-selling author of the MacLarens of Fire Mountain Series, the MacLarens of Boundary Mountain Series, and the Redemption Mountain Series. Shirleen grew up in Southern California, attended Oregon State University, and has degrees from San Diego State University and the University of Maryland. Her passion is writing emotionally charged stories of flawed people who find redemption through love and acceptance. She lives with her husband in a beautiful town in northern Arizona. Between them, they have five adult sons who are their greatest achievements.

I love to hear from my readers!

Send me an email: shirleen@shirleendavies.com
Visit my Website: www.shirleendavies.com
Sign up to be notified of New Releases:
www.shirleendavies.com
Check out all of my Books:
www.shirleendavies.com/books.html
Comment on my Blog:
www.shirleendavies.com/blog.html
Follow me on Amazon:
http://www.amazon.com/author/shirleendavies

Follow my on BookBub:
https://www.bookbub.com/authors/shirleen-davies

Other ways to connect with me:

Facebook Author Page:
http://www.facebook.com/shirleendaviesauthor
Twitter: www.twitter.com/shirleendavies
Pinterest: http://pinterest.com/shirleendavies
Instagram:
https://www.instagram.com/shirleendavies_author/
Google Plus:
https://plus.google.com/+ShirleenDaviesAuthor

Books by Shirleen Davies

Historical Western Romance Series
MacLarens of Fire Mountain

Tougher than the Rest, Book One
Faster than the Rest, Book Two
Harder than the Rest, Book Three
Stronger than the Rest, Book Four
Deadlier than the Rest, Book Five
Wilder than the Rest, Book Six

Redemption Mountain

Redemption's Edge, Book One
Wildfire Creek, Book Two
Sunrise Ridge, Book Three
Dixie Moon, Book Four
Survivor Pass, Book Five
Promise Trail, Book Six
Deep River, Book Seven
Courage Canyon, Book Eight
Forsaken Falls, Book Nine
Solitude Gorge, Book Ten
Rogue Rapids, Book Eleven, Coming next in the series!

MacLarens of Boundary Mountain

Colin's Quest, Book One,

Brodie's Gamble, Book Two
Quinn's Honor, Book Three
Sam's Legacy, Book Four
Heather's Choice, Book Five
Nate's Destiny, Book Six
Blaine's Wager, Book Seven
Fletcher's Pride, Book Eight, Coming next in the series!

Contemporary Romance Series

MacLarens of Fire Mountain

Second Summer, Book One
Hard Landing, Book Two
One More Day, Book Three
All Your Nights, Book Four
Always Love You, Book Five
Hearts Don't Lie, Book Six
No Getting Over You, Book Seven
'Til the Sun Comes Up, Book Eight
Foolish Heart, Book Nine
Forever Love, Book Ten, Coming next in the series!

Peregrine Bay

Reclaiming Love, Book One, A Novella
Our Kind of Love, Book Two

Burnt River

Shane's Burden, Book One by Peggy Henderson
Thorn's Journey, Book Two by Shirleen Davies
Aqua's Achilles, Book Three by Kate Cambridge
Ashley's Hope, Book Four by Amelia Adams
Harpur's Secret, Book Five by Kay P. Dawson
Mason's Rescue, Book Six by Peggy L. Henderson
Del's Choice, Book Seven by Shirleen Davies
Ivy's Search, Book Eight by Kate Cambridge
Phoebe's Fate, Book Nine by Amelia Adams
Brody's Shelter, Book Ten by Kay P. Dawson
Boone's Surrender, Book Eleven by Shirleen Davies
Watch for more books in the series!

The best way to stay in touch is to subscribe to my newsletter. Go to www.shirleendavies.com and subscribe in the box at the top of the right column that asks for your email. You'll be notified of new books before they are released, have chances to win great prizes, and receive other subscriber-only specials.

Made in the USA
Coppell, TX
17 August 2020

33524250R00167